MW01135245

GETTING IT IN THE END
G.A. HAUSER

Chapter One

"It's hot out. You want to just do a quick three miles?" Mark asked, changing into shorts and a T-shirt.

Steve stared at Mark as Mark sat on their bed to yank on a pair of socks. "That doesn't sound like very much." Steve stood, tucking in his shirt.

"Four?"

"Okay. Four. We'll save the long runs for the weekend."

"It's too bloody hot out." Mark found a rubber band on his nightstand and pulled his long hair back from his face.

Steve loved to ogle him. Just the sight of Mark Richfield got him hot. Now that he and Mark were running every day together, Steve looked forward to the sweaty after-run sex that followed the exercise.

He'd thought he'd tire of Mark, working at the same advertising agency and living with him. But that hadn't happened.

Once Mark had his Dodgers ball cap in place with his ponytail flowing out of the back, Steve couldn't ignore the attraction he felt for this man. He hauled Mark into a kiss. As he ground his hips into Mark's, he could feel that big dick rubbing against him. Even when Mark's cock wasn't fully erect, Steve's body lit on fire from the contact.

After he parted from the kiss, Mark chided, "Officer

Miller, if you keep that up, we'll be having sex before the run."

Steve knew Mark couldn't resist calling him "officer". He was an ex-LAPD cop and that turned Mark on. "Sorry, I couldn't resist." Steve forced himself to let go.

"Right. Shall we?" Mark led the way out of their bedroom while Steve salivated at the sight of his tight ass in tiny red shorts.

Outside Mark said, "Oh, I forgot to mention something to you."

"Yes, dear?" Steve asked playfully as they ran past rows of stately Bel Air homes with gated entries.

"You know that silly new account, Artists and Models for Hire?"

"That front for prostitution?"

"Steven, it isn't a front for prostitution." Mark paused at a corner, then tapped Steve to go when the cars cleared out.

"Sure it ain't."

"You think Parsons and Company would take their account if they weren't strictly above board?"

"Never mind." Steve ignored the comment. "What about them?"

"When I went there to talk them into some long-term advertising, the owner, Arnold Newhouse, just about begged me to do a photo shoot."

Steve groaned. "I thought you were dead set against modeling."

"Well, I was."

"But?"

"I thought it might be a pleasant diversion. I wouldn't take anything seriously. After that little guest spot I did on *Forever Young*, I have to admit I got a taste of being in the spotlight and I liked it."

"Vanity, vanity…" Steve teased, increasing the speed of

2

his pace.

"Are you running deliberately fast to lose me?"

"To punish you." Steve gave him a sly glance.

"Stop it or I'll leave you in the dust."

Steve slowed down slightly, knowing Mark was much faster in a sprint than he was. "So? Now you suddenly want to model? Is this a career change, or in addition to Parsons."

"No. Not a career change. Just for fun."

"You're jealous of Angel Loveday." Steve was thinking about the hot porn star of the old eighties films they had befriended.

"You do say the most unbelievable things."

"I just don't understand this sudden need to be photographed."

"I did it before. You remember that male nude coffee table book? *American Male-Men*?"

"How could I forget? Larsen has like ten copies." Steve could never repress a twinge of jealousy at the thought of Jack Larsen, who had been Mark's best friend for two decades.

"Two. He has two."

"Look, you want me to take some naked shots of you, stick them on the web and expose your nice big cock for you?"

"Shut up, Steven."

"Hey, now look who's increasing the pace. Slow the fuck down or we'll never make it four miles."

"I didn't say they'd be pornographic. Why do you have such a perverted mind?"

"Because I've seen you naked, and if I were to take photos of you, they'd be showing your lusciously large male anatomy."

"Not all models show off their privates. I was thinking more of headshots anyway." Mark adjusted the brim of his cap in the sun's glare.

"You do what you like. If you think it'll be fun, go for it."

"Thank you. That's all I wanted to hear."

Steve stuck his hand on Mark's ass.

Mark glanced back to look at him in exasperation. "You're trying to make me trip."

"No, I'm trying to cop a feel."

"You'll get your feel later, copper."

"Mm, can't fucking wait."

Mark laughed at him until the pace began to get more grueling.

Mark couldn't breathe, they were running so hard. Whenever they neared their home on the last leg of their run, they tended to race to the finish. After four miles of boiling heat and a pace much faster than Mark would have liked, Steve bolted to the front of the house, competitive in every way.

Mark let up before they both smacked into the front door to "tag" the finish line. He halted on the walkway leading up to their four-bedroom split-level, allowing Steve to slap the wood and win. Still gasping for air, Mark leaned over his knees to catch his breath.

"Son of a bitch, it's hot." Steve untied his key from his shoelace.

The sweat began to sting Mark's eyes, so he took off his cap and sunglasses and mopped up his face with his drenched T-shirt. "You always have to make it into a competition."

"I have to be better than you at something, Richfield." Steve pushed back the door and they both groaned with relief at the air-conditioned coolness.

Mark removed two bottles of water from the refrigerator, handing one to Steve and gulping his. Finally able to breathe normally, Mark took off his shirt to soak up the sweat that continued to pour out of him as he cooled down.

Steve flicked his tongue over Mark's exposed nipple.

Mark raised his eyebrow at the gesture, inspecting the demonic expression on his lover's face. "Give me a minute. I'm not twenty any longer."

"Maybe not, but you have the body of a twenty-year-old." Steve hugged Mark, licking the slow-moving drops of sweat from Mark's chest. "You weren't too old for an orgy with Keith and Carl."

"Oh, that," Mark moaned. "I think my multiple-partner days are over. It was fun, but…"

"But?" Steve sucked one of his nipples, biting it between his lip-covered teeth.

"I just want you, Officer Miller. I think thirty-seven is too old to be playing around like that."

Steve paused, leaning back to meet Mark's gaze. "Really?"

"Yes, love. Really." Mark finished the water in his bottle and tossed it into the kitchen sink. Steve had his arms wrapped around his waist, preventing him from going anywhere.

"Is that why you want to do this modeling thing? Because you're getting older?"

Mark flinched, hating to admit it. He lowered his eyelashes. "I won't be attractive forever, Steve. Once I'm old, what will be left of me but memories of my looks?"

Steve met his eyes. "There's more to you than your beauty."

Mark laughed sadly. "Sure there is. And you would have been attracted to my personality if I looked different."

"Cut this shit out." Steve shook his shoulders. "Do you think I'm so shallow that all I want you for is your body?"

A sharp pain seared through Mark's chest. He knew he was an emotional mess. If it wasn't for his sex appeal, he'd be alone.

"Mark?"

"Let me shower. I'm hot." Mark turned away from Steve's

irritated expression. He climbed the stairs to their bedroom and stood next to their bed, shedding the rest of his clothing and leaving it in a damp pile. He could hear Steve undressing behind him. Mark stepped into the bathroom. Before he turned on the shower, he peeked at the mirror.

He caught his own gaze. Bright green irises framed by thick dark lashes. While he kept his attention on his reflection, he took the rubber band out of his hair. He combed through its damp, sweaty length, feeling it brush the nape of his neck and shoulders.

With his palms on the sink, he leaned and stared critically at his features. He'd been compared to a woman his whole life, called pretty, fag, androgynous, Ganymede, and everything under the sun to slam whatever was left of his manhood. His father had been abusive. Being an only child, Mark had to bear the brunt of all Milt Richfield's anger and frustration. No matter what Mark had achieved, his dominating father never saw fit to praise him.

Mark heard Steve come into the room behind him.

"What's going on, Mark?" Steve rocked him gently.

In frustration Mark bit his lip as he fought for a way to explain how he felt. He exhaled a deep breath. "Steven, I feel like Dorian Gray. That everything I've done in my life will turn me into what I really am inside."

"And what are you inside?" Steve kissed Mark's neck.

"Ugly."

Steve spun him around so they were facing each other.

"You are not ugly, Mark. Far from it. You're loving, kind and sweet."

"You're biased because you're attracted to my looks."

"What's brought all this on?" Steve toyed with Mark's long hair.

"There's too much going through my mind at the moment."

"Can I help? Do you want to talk about it?"

"No." Mark attempted to break the embrace to get to the shower. Steve held him firm.

"Why do I get the feeling this is all coming on the heels of that sex we had with Keith and Carl?"

Steve had it dead on. What Steve didn't know was that Mark had had a three-way with those men the day before all four of them got together. In other words, he'd cheated on Steve and had only brought him in on the event later to appease his guilt. Not only that, but Keith O'Leary had manipulated Steve to allow Mark to do a guest appearance on their late-night cable television drama, *Forever Young*.

Mark was furious with himself. Ego. Ego and pride had once again led him down the wrong path. And now he was living to regret it. He couldn't stop himself. He had allowed those two men to lure him into a three-way. What the hell was wrong with him? *Are you that flamin' insecure, Richfield?*

Yes.

Did it matter how many people thought he was pretty? No. He lapped up the compliments even though he never took them to heart. The admirers who spoke those flattering words didn't "know" the real him. Any man could look decent if the secret of his nasty personality was hidden.

"Mark?"

"Let me shower." Mark reached into the stall and turned on the taps. As he did, Steve ran kisses down his neck and shoulders. Mark held back the tears, knowing he didn't deserve a man as wonderful as Steven Jay Miller.

The more Steve adored him the more anger Mark felt. He was a lying piece of shit. Couldn't everyone see that? He didn't deserve love.

While Mark wet down under the spraying head, Steve pulled leisurely on his own cock. He grew hard. The sight of

Mark, his tall, sleek body, his flawless bronze skin, and large male anatomy hanging low between his legs always excited him. Yes, Mark's looks were a complete turn-on, but if Mark were nasty and conceited, those looks would mean nothing. Mark Antonious Richfield was as soft and voluptuous as a woman on the inside. Feline eyes and movements, shiny long, thick hair, and the biggest dick Steve had ever seen on a man, Mark was everything Steve wanted and more.

And he wanted him now.

Steve knelt between Mark's legs, opened his lips and allowed Mark's soft penis into his mouth. The water from the shower ran down Mark's golden skin and against Steve's face.

Steve knew Mark was capable of the cruelest self-inflicted punishment. Mark didn't know Steve was aware of that, but he was. It wasn't rocket science. Yes, Mark had great beauty and charm, but that always came with a price. And the price of Mark's appeal was his self-hatred and insecurity. If you didn't know that about Mark, then you knew nothing about him.

It only made Steve more protective of Mark, more the pit bull to keep him safe, sound and at peace. He was indulgent. So? It was his business. What Mark wanted, Steve made sure he got. Mark's happiness was Steve's number-one concern. Period. And if that meant giving into Mark's desires, so be it.

Steve drew Mark's cock completely inside his mouth. It pulsated and grew. His eyes closed as the water pelted his face. Steve wrapped his right hand around Mark's hips and toyed with his heavy sack with his other.

A low groan echoed off the wet tiles. Once Mark was completely erect Steve wouldn't be able to fit Mark's cock entirely inside his mouth.

Steve remembered Keith O'Leary, that sexy, blue-eyed blond superstar sucking Mark's cock and Carl Bronson, Keith's muscular, brunette co-star, enveloping Mark's balls. That happened while Steve clasped his hands at the base of Mark's cock at the same time to make Mark shiver and come. Just thinking about that incident caused Steve to whimper in excitement and his dick to bob in yearning.

Those two handsome actors had wanted Mark so badly they had seduced Steve just so he would agree. How many men had tried to seduce Mark and failed? As far as Steve knew, it was just he, Keith and Carl who had tasted Mark's cock. Jack Larsen, Mark's best friend all through college, had craved it since they played baseball together, but Jack never had it. *Poor Jack, you don't know what you're missing.*

Moaning louder than Mark, Steve gripped the base of Mark's long shaft in two hands and drew as hard as he could on it to the tip, sliding it as deeply as he dared into his throat. He tasted Mark's pre-come on his tongue. Steve was lucky to have found Mark. He'd stolen Mark away from Sharon Tice, snatched him from the altar on their wedding day, mid-vows. And now Mark was his. Not Jack's, not Sharon's, not Keith's, not Carl's, but his.

And Steve was as possessive as a dog with his favorite bone. Possessive and defensive. As an ex-LAPD cop, Steve wanted to protect and serve one man, 'til his death.

Mark's gasps always sent shivers down Steve's spine. Increasing his speed and suction, Steve reached between Mark's legs, found his tight ring and pushed in.

Those delicious whimpering cries, *Ah! Ah!* sent Steve wild. A vibrating throbbing rattled Mark's long cock and Steve began swallowing down the load, groaning and closing his eyes tighter at the taste and quantity of Mark's come. Steve could live on his knees before this man and be happy.

Mark braced himself on the tile and shower door and felt the reverberation of the orgasm rock his body. Before he could recover, Steve spun him to face the wall and shoved his dick up Mark's ass. Mark closed his eyes. Steve's soapy cock slid in deep and fast. Mark shivered at the penetration, loving Steve's body inside his.

Mark went numb from the overload to his senses. He loved his macho ex-LAPD tough guy and knew what Steve wanted. An alpha male in every way, Steve was the top to Mark's bottom exclusively. And Mark would have it no other way.

He loved getting it in the end, loved it. Playing submissive to this amazing, masculine man was pure fantasy. Why he would do anything to jeopardize it, he didn't know.

Steve never took long. He used to learn tricks to hold back so he could please Sonja Knight, his attorney ex-girlfriend. It didn't matter anymore. Steve could spurt in one second. Mark didn't need him to stay hard to come, not like a woman. Though knowing that, Mark didn't want Steve to pull out either. The heat, the connection and the unity made him feel whole. When Steve was inside him, he felt worthy.

Steve thrust his hips, slapping them against Mark's wet bottom and climaxed, his deep grunting echoing in the steamy room. With Steve's weight nailing him to the wall, Mark closed his eyes. It was the only time he was at peace.

Gently, Steve disconnected from Mark's body, holding Mark's hips as he did.

"I love you," Steve said seductively.

That made Mark smile. He always heard an "I love you" after Steve fucked him. Maybe it was Steve's way of thanking him.

As a tease, Mark replied, "You're welcome."

There was no jovial laugh in response. Steve urged Mark to turn around physically by his waist.

Mark wasn't prepared for the anguish in Steve's expression. "What did I do now?"

"Nothing. Get over here." Steve embraced him, kissing Mark deeply. When Steve parted from Mark's lips, he whispered, "Don't worry. Whatever it is you're thinking about, don't let it upset you."

Mark stared at his hero, his savior, and whispered back, "I

do love you. You know that."

Steve gripped Mark's jaw roughly. "I know."

Chapter Two

The alarm set for seven, Mark lay still, staring at the ceiling as Steve nestled against him in the dark. Steve's hand lightly cupped Mark's crotch, the way it did each night, as if Steve were claiming that piece of him, or protecting it. Mark wasn't sure which and didn't mind either scenario. It was part of their nightly routine. After washing up, they cuddled the same way, Steve crushed against his side with a hand sheltering his private parts from the demons of the night.

Steve tended to fall asleep first while Mark struggled with his own set of demons.

The comfort of Steve's deep, restful respirations usually lulled Mark to the unconscious, but not tonight.

It was more of the same agony that plagued him.

Jack had seen the clip on YouTube. Actually, Jack had seen the front page of the *Inspirer*.

Me in bed between Keith and Carl.

It was a scene from *Forever Young*, and Mark wanted to convince Jack that that was all it was. TV. He would die if Jack knew he, or he and Steve, had had group sex with those two studs.

Poor Jack.

It seemed no matter what Mark did, Jack got the fallout. Mark's guilt for breaking Jack's heart would never vanish. Guilt from attempting to marry Sharon and then—worse—falling in love with Steve during a business retreat in New Mexico would never vanish. Jack had loved him since they met at Stanford University and played baseball together.

That first year they became friends, Mark was so attracted to that big, brawny blond he had a horrible time resisting him. But that was when Mark was still in denial. The cock teasing Mark had done to that poor man was criminal.

Mark dabbed at a tear that threatened, moving slowly so as not to wake Steve.

Obviously, it wasn't meant to be. One taste of Steve Miller's tongue and Mark was addicted to men, permanently.

At least Jack had Adam.

When he thought of Adam making love to his Jack—yes, *his* "Jackie" or "Jackie-blue"—Mark cringed. Likewise, Jack was insanely jealous of Steve. What would Jack do if he knew Mark had had sex with someone other than Steve?

And not him?

Put simply, Jack would go ballistic.

According to Adam, Jack had already arrived at "ballistic" and was refusing Mark's phone calls. They were back to square one again...Jack cutting Mark out of his life the way he had done just months ago when Mark moved in with Steve. Mark didn't want to relive the anguish of begging, stalking, forcing Jack to forgive him.

Mark couldn't deal with the silent treatment, the shunning again. Just when he thought he'd won Jack's friendship back, this tabloid story had appeared.

A deep, torturous sob threatened. Mark bit his lip as hard as he could to hold it in.

I hate myself for the pain I've inflicted on you, Jack. You are the kindest, most generous man I know. And I've done nothing but hurt you. He could imagine Jack's expression of betrayal.

13

Mark broke down. He had no resources to deal with any of this. Steve put up with so much from him already, and Mark just didn't want to burden him anymore. So he tried to stop the anguish, but it was making him a total wreck. He couldn't feel any more miserable than he already did.

Slowly coming to the surface from a deep sleep, Steve heard the sound of Mark crying, sat up and checked the clock. It was nearing midnight. "Babe?"

In the dimness Mark raised his hands from under the sheets to cover his face. Steve drew closer to him in alarm, wrapping his arms around him. "Mark? What happened? Did you have a bad dream?"

Mark didn't answer, but his weeping intensified.

Steve clutched him tighter. "What is going on in that beautiful head of yours, Richfield? Talk to me."

He dragged Mark's hands from his face. Mark's tears deepened to a body-wracking wail. In agony, Steve sealed Mark against him, petting his hair and kissing him, cooing softly, "Hush, all right…stop crying, please."

While he rocked Mark, feeling his own emotions begin to crack at the sound of so much heartache, Steve knew this had something to do with the experience they had with Keith and Carl; he just didn't know why.

Slowly Mark's sobs softened. Steve wiped Mark's damp hair from his face, drying his tears. He kissed his coarse jaw, tasted the saltiness of his lips and caressed him, trying to comfort him. "Please let out what's inside you. Don't bottle it up."

"You'll hate me. Jack will hate me. I'm horrible."

"I won't hate you. This is about Keith and Carl, isn't it?"

"Yes."

"Mark, we won't do it again with them. Okay? Did you get upset with what we did?"

14

Steve had a feeling what the three of them did to Mark was too much. Geez, they'd treated him like a frickin' pincushion. Everyone wanted to be inside him. Mark had been taking it from both ends at one point and, though he'd appeared to be enjoying it, maybe he hadn't been. Steve knew damn well he, himself, wouldn't do it—suck a cock and get fucked simultaneously. It was degrading as far as he was concerned. But he thought Mark loved playing the submissive. Maybe not. Maybe the memory of that event was making Mark feel cheated.

Mark tried to turn over, to face away from Steve.

"What the hell is so bad? Just say it." Steve struggled to keep Mark on his back as Mark began to curl into the fetal position. "Let's call in sick tomorrow," Steve offered.

"No."

"Mark." Steve ran his hand over Mark's chest. "It was wrong of us to screw you like that. I suppose we all got carried away."

"That's not it."

"Then what is? Is it because Jack found out?"

"Yes."

About to roll his eyes and release a deep sigh, Steve dug his hand through Mark's hair to reassure him. "You can't keep beating yourself up for everything you do in your life that upsets Larsen. Forget about it."

Mark spun back again to confront him. Steve almost jumped, the movement was so abrupt. "I cheated on you."

That comment totally caught Steve off guard. An ice ball filled his stomach. "With whom? Jack?"

"No."

Steve knelt up and glared at Mark. "With whom?"

"The night before we had our foursome, I did it with Keith and Carl."

Steve's brain went into overdrive, trying to think about

15

what he was hearing. "You'd already had sex with those two when you asked me to join you?"

"Yes." Mark flinched back as if he were going to get slapped.

"Mark!" Steve couldn't help but feel sick.

"Baby…forgive me."

Steve climbed out of bed, grabbed his pillow and headed out of the room. He didn't know what this meant to them as a couple, but he needed some time to think about it.

"Steve!" Mark rushed him, gripping his arm. "Don't leave. Don't do this."

"Don't do this?" Steve jerked back his arm. "Get away from me."

Mark recoiled as if he had been kicked.

Steve walked out, trying to decide just how angry he was.

Mark fell to his knees on the floor. No one should have to put up with him. No one. His father was right. He was a worthless piece of shit.

He didn't know what was worse, cheating on Steve or being stupid enough to tell him.

No. I had to tell him. I'm going mad.

Mark brushed at the tears that fell from his eyes. He glanced at the telephone on the nightstand, thinking of calling Jack for advice. But that was ludicrous, Jack despised him at the moment. So that left no one. No one to comfort the loser who inflicted damage on the ones he loved. Mark knew in his very core he must be selfish and greedy. How anyone tolerated him, he didn't know.

No wonder he'd been used constantly for his looks. It didn't pay to get close to him. Look how he treated the ones he loved most?

"Just kill me," he moaned, feeling his heart beating

forcefully. He had images of leaving, going far away, abandoning the people he seemed to harm on a constant basis so they would finally be rid of him, rid of the nuisance. Mark imagined taking a flight to someplace desolate and becoming a recluse. He couldn't keep causing this kind of pain to Jack and Steve. It was killing him, and his beloved men.

Unable to contain his anguish, Mark curled into a ball and struggled to deal with it by himself. The words of his dead father telling him how soft and useless he was were battling with the tiny voice in his head that begged him not to do anything foolish to himself. Or better yet, beg forgiveness.

Chapter Three

Steve threw his pillow on the bed in the guest room. Without turning the spread down, he flopped back on it and stewed. Tricked. He'd been tricked. There was nothing he hated worse than being made a fool.

He'd suffered already from his relationship with Mark. Steve's parents were completely ignorant of it, and he constantly pretended he was straight and too busy to date. It was infuriating. But if his racist, homophobic, ex-police sergeant father had hated him dating an African American woman, then Dick Miller would go crazy at Steve's new beau. Pretty, androgynous Mark Antonious.

Steve turned over and punched the pillow. Hadn't he always known Mark would cheat? How could he be enough for a man as sexual as Mark? Obviously, he wasn't.

Manipulated. He'd been manipulated by those two actors. That whole ruse when Keith and Carl dressed in police uniforms and gave him the ultimate pat down, that was all to get Mark into their beds again. It had nothing to do with him. And the insult to his pride was substantial.

"Baby?"

Steve turned to the door.

Mark's naked, seraphic form was lit from the outside street lamp's glow shining through the windowpane. Even in that dim light, Steve could see how exceptional Mark was.

"Forgive me?"

Could he blame those two men for wanting a piece of that? No. Did he blame Mark for accepting the invitation? *Yes.*

"Love?"

Mark's lithe figure floated closer. His body was such a cross between male and female it drove Steve crazy. Mark didn't have the typical powerful male frame. He was so tall and slender, his legs seemed to go on forever, and his shoulders, though they were broad, weren't muscle-bound. That ridiculously long head of thick brown hair only added to the gender enigma.

Steve didn't want to go into heat whenever Mark entered a room. It just happened.

Mark seemed to glide across the carpet towards him. When he paused at the side of the bed, his genitals were at Steve's eye level. And that didn't help Steve remain rational.

Then came the seduction, Mark smoothing both his hands down his body to his crotch. Steve knew damn well no one played the sex card quite as well as Mark Richfield. Mark used sex to get everything he wanted.

Steve knew why. Mark didn't think he possessed any other worthwhile qualities. It was absurd. Mark was brilliant, funny, loving, generous, all the things that made the perfect partner. But Mark didn't believe he had all those traits. Milt Richfield had been thorough in making his son feel useless and self-conscious. Milt's degrading battles about Mark's sexuality and self-esteem had left his son scarred for life.

Mark gathered up that magnificent set of male genitalia into his hands and offered it to Steve. He'd done that before, when Steve was trying to get over Mark as Mark's wedding loomed. Mark had stood in his hotel room, naked, his hands gathering up those heavy testicles and ridiculously large cock, bargaining with his body.

Steve's own dick was rigid. *Mark, you SOB. You do it to me every time.*

"Why?" Steve tore his gaze from that delicious prick to Mark's eyes. "Why did you go with them?"

"I'm weak. I'm ashamed of the reasons."

"Tell me."

Mark crouched next to him. "Vanity. Ego. Insecurity?"

"Did you ever go out on me before?"

"No. Never."

Steve studied Mark's eyes, like a cop trying to beat out a confession. "Why did you wait so long to tell me?"

Mark made a gesture with his hands as if stating it was obvious.

"As you grow older," Steve asked, "and you become more insecure about your looks, will it happen more and more?"

"No. Never. Cross my heart and hope to die." Mark drew an *X* on his chest.

"Is this what you've been beating yourself up with for the past week? Your guilt about it?"

"Yes. About you and about Jack."

Jack again. Steve couldn't imagine Mark not thinking about Jack's wellbeing. It was hard not to be jealous of that as well, but Jack and Adam were happy and exclusive.

Mark leaned over the bed and caressed Steve's hair. At the touch of his hands, Steve's body responded, his cock moving in earnest, nodding between his legs.

"Come back to our bed. Please. I know I'm a terrible person and I have no right to someone as wonderful as you." Mark dragged his fingers over Steve's rigid length teasingly. "But you must forgive me, lover. Or I will truly go mad."

Even if Steve's mind said no, his body never turned down Mark's offers. Steve rolled off the mattress, picked Mark up, threw him over his shoulder roughly, grabbed his pillow, and headed back to their bedroom. Once he was beside his own bed, he tossed Mark down on it with his pillow and stared at him. Without having to ask, Mark got to his hands and knees and began sucking Steve's cock.

Steve gripped Mark's hair in tight fists and fucked his mouth. His legs tensing, arching his back to thrust out his pelvis, Steve knew he'd never break up with Mark or even stay angry at him. The love and attraction he felt for him were eternal in nature. If Steve ever lost him, he would die. Literally.

Not only that, but he knew Mark. Mark was not stable. And with Jack giving him the silent treatment at the moment, Mark had no one. Steve had a feeling that without someone to love him, Mark would do something desperate and terrible to himself. Without love, Mark would not survive. And he sure as shit didn't get any from his aloof British mother, that much Steve did know. They never called each other. Never. Since that horrible incident in the wedding hall when Mark ran up the aisle to Steve, leaving Sharon behind, Leslie had ignored her son.

Mark's seductive groan brought Steve to the edge. Mark loved to play submissive to the extreme. Tied up, handcuffed, fucked raw, Mark couldn't get enough. Steve's own cock wasn't quite the size of Mark's so he forced it completely into Mark's mouth, feeling his tip brush Mark's throat. His balls tightened and the pleasure began squirming through them as they churned up their load, He strengthened his hold on Mark, pressed him closer and started to rise. Mark gripped Steve's ass in both hands and yanked him forward, causing Steve's cock to completely penetrate his mouth.

Richfield's mouth. There was nothing quite like it. And the pleasure and hunger Mark had for sucking cock was insatiable.

When a deep grunt of pleasure passed his lips as the climax hit, Steve held Mark in place to make damn sure he swallowed every frickin' drop. Yeah, maybe it was punishment for the lies, but Steve knew this type of punishment Mark could handle. Being left to stew on his own would only torment a soul that was already inflicting self-destruction.

"Suck it, Richfield. Suck it fucking good," Steve crooned, giving a few more deep thrusts into Mark's mouth. "That's it, baby." He caressed Mark's long thick hair.

This was all Mark had to do to feel he was forgiven. Steve knew Mark. It was one way Mark coped with the tangle he always seemed to create around himself. Give sex as penance. And Steve was happy to receive it. So it was a bonus blowjob.

Even though he'd been sucked dry, Steve allowed him to continue as long as he desired. As Steve gazed down at the act, he had to smile. *Look at him. Christ, he's in heaven.* Mark's brows were furrowed in deep pleasure. Little whimpering moans, which sent chills up Steve's spine, echoed in the dim room. The love Steve felt for Mark, particularly at the height of orgasm, consumed him. The sight of Mark's bliss in having given Steve a good one was certainly forgiveness enough for both of them.

Mark inhaled Steve's masculine scent in delight. Steve's pubic hair tickled the skin of his face as he took his cock deep. When the hot spunk hit his tongue, Mark closed his eyes and swallowed in awe. While Steve's body pulsated in his mouth it was pure heaven. Mark sucked out every last bit, milking it thoroughly before he released it from his mouth. When he did, Steve nudged him to move over, dropping heavily beside him. Without a word, Steve closed his eyes and went back to sleep. Mark nestled in next to him, bringing Steve's hand against his balls where it should be.

After a deep exhale, trying to feel some relief, Mark felt as if one problem was behind him. He had one more to go. Jack Larsen.

Chapter Four

A cup of coffee in his hand, Mark sat at the kitchen table with the cordless phone. "Adam? Is Jack there?"

"Hi, Mark. He's here but he doesn't want to talk to you."

"Please. Please just hand him the phone." Mark felt a lump in his throat. He heard Adam telling Jack to take it.

A moment later Adam said, "I'm sorry, Mark."

Burning tears stung Mark's eyes. "Adam, what should I do? Tell him it was for the show. Convince him."

After a deep, exhaled breath, Adam replied, "To be honest, Mark, I don't want to get involved and be the go-between for you guys."

"No. Of course. I understand."

"I have to go, Mark."

"Yes. Bye." Mark hung up and set the phone on the table in front of him. They were back at square one. Jack ignoring him. Mark couldn't stand it.

Steve caressed Mark's hair from behind. "No luck?"

"No. He despises me."

"Look, stop living your life to please a man you can't please."

For some reason Mark instantly thought of the parallel of that comment to his father. History was repeating itself.

"Let's go." Steve tapped Mark's arm.

Mark stood and set his mug in the sink, following Steve to the front door.

Once he was sitting next to Steve in the passenger's seat of his Mercedes, Mark remembered his college days when he and Jack first met. He even recalled dragging Jack out on a double date. They were roommates in a tiny apartment just off the campus, both of them living off handouts from their parents. The apartment was a tiny, rough—practically devoid of furniture—two-bedroom. It had been impossible to get any privacy in that place.

With the constant echo of his father's accusations burning in his ears, Mark had arranged for two women to go out for a drink and quick bite to eat with them. Mark recollected Jack being behind the wheel of his rusty Ford Taurus, his date trying without luck to seduce him and Mark's date groping and gnawing at him in the backseat. They had finished eating and were parked in front of the girls' sorority house. While Stephanie pressed Mark against the interior door, Mark had opened his eyes to see Jack staring at him, watching as Stephanie kissed him.

It had been cruel punishment for both of them. But Mark would be damned if he'd prove all his father's accusations to be true. He was not a weak faggot. Over-mothered. Spoiled. Feminine.

"You okay?" Steve shook Mark's leg.

"Hm? Yes." Those memories haunted Mark. It got worse. Mark remembered Jack's eyes on him constantly in that apartment. Though Jack never admitted it, never "came out" to him, Mark had felt the attraction for and from Jack.

In the heat of late spring, Mark slept nude. Jack would come into his room early on the pretext of rousing him for class or baseball practice. On more than one occasion, Mark would wake to find Jack gazing down at him while he slept.

Steve parked in his assigned spot at Parsons and Company.

Once he had shut off the ignition, he twisted to face Mark, running his hand through Mark's hair. "He'll come around. Just give him time."

"I don't know." Mark wondered how many cheeks Jack had left to turn.

"Just don't stalk him. That didn't get you anywhere last time."

Mark had a craving to do just that. Seek Jack out, beg his forgiveness. Jack meant way too much to him to allow this wall of silence to remain.

After a quick kiss on Mark's cheek, Steve exited the car with his briefcase, pausing as Mark did the same.

"Yes. It did work, Steven. I wore him down. Remember? The day he called you to give Adam lessons in shooting?"

"I remember. I also remember him getting angry when we kept dropping by unannounced. Will you give him some time?"

"No." Steve should know him better than that. Mark was not a patient man. Quite the contrary.

"Behave, Richfield."

A wry smile on his lips, Mark repeated, "No."

Once they were on their way to the elevator, Steve wrapped his arm around Mark's back and held him tight. A deep sigh escaping his lips, Mark leaned against him heavily. The stress was depleting him of energy and now he constantly felt tired. He could nap against Steve where they stood.

When the elevator doors opened to their lobby, Mark had to stand up straight and walk on his own.

An hour later, Steve caught Mark as he passed his office. "Where are you off to?"

"I've an appointment downtown."

"Need the keys?"

"No. I'll take one of the company cars."

"You sure?" Steve dangled the key ring.

"Do you have any appointments?" Mark entered his office.

"Not until after lunch."

Mark thought about it. "No. I'll use one of the spare cars. Thanks, Steve."

"Mark?" Steve stood and, brushing up against him, he rubbed Mark's arm through his suit jacket. He purred softly, "You okay?"

"I'm fine, love," Mark lied.

"Let's do something special tonight."

Mark knew it was Steve's attempt at distracting him. "Yes. All right."

"Good." Steve pecked Mark's lips and stood back.

"See you soon." Mark gave Steve his best smile and headed down the hall to get the car keys from one of the secretaries.

Outside Mark located the black sedan. He sat down behind the wheel and started it up to get the air conditioning running, opening the windows in the meantime. Quickly checking his face in the rearview mirror, he pushed his hair back from his eyes and fastened his seatbelt.

The traffic was brutal. In frustration Mark drummed his fingers on the steering wheel. He glanced at his watch nervously. Finally arriving at his destination, he found a pay lot and took the ticket from the machine, stuffing it into his suit jacket.

Outside the dim parking garage, in the glaring sunlight, Mark removed his sunglasses from his pocket and put them on his face. He felt as if the pressure of the world was upon him. He walked with the flow of pedestrians across the street when the traffic signal changed.

After he entered the lobby of a high-rise building, he removed his sunglasses and felt the cool air with relief. A brief ride in the elevator and he stood before a glass window with the words "Bernstein, Larsen, Knight, and Associates" written on it.

He stopped before entering. There were several reasons he had never visited Jack at work before. One was because Steve's ex-girlfriend worked with him. Sonja Knight. Mark had never met her and had only heard of her in snippets of what Steve would relay about their relationship. Yes, Mark had been curious to meet her, see what she was like, but he hadn't had the nerve.

Mark wanted to believe the past had no bearing on the present, but he knew that was a lie. The past was everything.

"They're all probably in court," he muttered to himself. As he tried to compose himself, smoothing his hair back before entering, he had no idea why he was doing this other than to beg Jack to speak to him. History kept repeating itself and he never learned from it. They say those who do not learn are destined to that fate. Mark was the worst student on the planet if that was the criteria. He'd only learned one thing in life. He needed his friends to love him or he'd die.

A receptionist raised her head from her phones at his entrance. He pretended he was fine and smiled at her, waiting for her to complete her call.

"Yes? Can I help you?"

"Is Jack Larsen in his office?"

"Do you have an appointment?"

"No."

"Oh. Yes, I think he is. Let me tell him you're here. May I have your name?"

Mark froze. He knew damn well if Jack heard he was here, he would tell this woman he was too busy to see him.

"My name..." Mark faltered. "Angel Loveday." If this woman had any knowledge of those old eighties soft-porn Plimpton/Loveday movies, he'd be caught. She appeared to be only in her twenties and when she didn't blink at the name of the famous star, Mark knew he was damn lucky.

Why had lying become so easy for him lately? *Oh yes, that's right. Years of practice living at Richfield manor,* he chided himself.

"Fine, Mr. Loveday. Could you have a seat?"

Mark felt ill. His entire life was a charade. He should be an actor, Keith was right. He was already pretending to be confident and whole; he might as well get paid for it.

Unable to sit because his insides were twisting, Mark gazed at the original artwork in the lobby with little interest. At the sound of Jack's voice, Mark spun around.

When Jack met his eyes, his pleasant demeanor dropped. "What do you want?"

"Jack, please." Mark instantly felt that dry lump in his throat.

As if Jack wanted to shout something rude, his lip curled in disgust.

Mark died at the hatred in his glare. "Please..." He would get on his hands and knees if he had to. He had no pride and would grovel to get Jack to hear him out.

Jack glanced at the receptionist, who was watching their every move. He spun on his heels and walked back down the hall. Mark raced after him.

Just before Mark entered Jack's office, he bumped into a gorgeous African American woman and knew it must be Sonja.

"Excuse me." She smiled sweetly and stepped aside. "Can I help you?"

"I...I'm..." Mark pointed to Jack's office. The knowledge that this stunning woman had made love to his Steve was killing him.

"Are you all right?" She touched Mark's arm.

"You...you're Sonja Knight, right?"

"Yes. And who are you? Have we met?"

When she extended her hand, Mark reached for it, clasping it firmly. "I'm Mark Richfield."

At the mention of his name, Sonja almost jerked back from the contact and inspected him closely. Perhaps she knew about the pain he had inflicted on Jack. Who knew what Jack had told her?

"Oh." She released his hand after a quick, polite shake.

Mark seemed to be unwelcome in so many places he felt like a criminal. They had nothing to say to each other. What were they supposed to do? Compare notes on Steve?

"If you'll excuse me." Sonja kept her poise and walked by him.

Mark cringed, feeling the slight like a blow. He touched the doorframe to steady himself. When he looked up, Jack was glaring at him from behind his desk.

"What the hell do you want?"

As if he had weights on his feet, Mark forced his legs to move, closing the door behind him for privacy. "To beg your forgiveness."

"Again?" Jack snarled. "Forget it, Mark. I don't give a shit who you fuck."

Mark knew that was bullshit. If Jack didn't care, why was he so angry?

"It was for a scene in their television show." Mark hated lying to him, but didn't think he had any choice. "They invited me to guest star on *Forever Young*. It was a threesome for the show. You know how the reporters of those tabloids twist things."

Jack glowered at him. "Do I look stupid?"

Mark stood, holding onto the back of a chair that was placed in front of the desk. He needed to sit down, but had a feeling Jack would instantly jump to his feet to get away from him. "No, Jack. You aren't stupid. Far from it."

29

"What do you want from me? Why can't you leave me the hell alone?"

"I can't. I need you."

"Get over it." Jack turned to his computer but didn't make a move to touch the keyboard.

"Love, please." An uncontrollable tidal wave began to move over him and he dreaded it. He tried to bridge the gap between them, praying Jack wouldn't bolt. "You know how much you mean to me. We've been here before. About Steven, remember? We managed to get through it." Mark had made it beside Jack's desk, closing in on him as Jack sat in a daze. "I hate upsetting you, Jackie. I can't sleep at night."

"Why do you give a shit? That's what I don't get."

Mark finally stood next to him. Now he was close enough to touch Jack. "Almost twenty years we've been friends. That's too much to give up on. And I never will." He caught the scent of Jack's cologne and assumed Jack could get a sniff of his as well. Mark crouched down alongside him as Jack reclined in the leather chair behind his desk. "Love, stop blaming me for everything I do. I've never been sensible. You were the sensible one of the two of us." Mark rested his hand on Jack's leg.

Instantly, Jack stared down at it. "Why are you touching me?"

"You know the answer to that." Mark was always amazed at the size of Jack's body. The man was so powerfully built he was Atlas come to life.

As if something broke inside of Jack, he breathed bitterly. "It seems everyone is allowed to have you but me."

"No. Nonsense." Mark smoothed his hand along Jack's thigh. "Only Steve. I swear to you."

"The YouTube video showed you, Keith and Carl kissing and writhing all over each other naked, Mark."

"For the taping. We did that for the show. Some moron who had it in for Keith and Carl videotaped us during a shoot.

You know all about what the producers of that show did to them. Ask Adam."

Jack rubbed his face tiredly. A voice came through his intercom, "Jack? You have a call on line one."

He hit a button on the machine. "I'll call back. Take a message."

Mark reached for Jack's hand and held it against his chest. "You know how much I love you. Please stop creating barriers between us."

Jack tugged out of Mark's grip. Mark felt miserable, until Jack used that hand to cup his face. At the tender touch, Mark immediately met Jack's turquoise eyes.

"I still love you." Jack's voice was shaky and soft.

The urge Mark had to crawl onto Jack's lap and kiss him was almost too strong to bear. His luck, Sonja would spy it and call Steve, and Mark would be back in the doghouse again.

"I wish I was allowed to love two men and be with them." Mark dabbed at the corner of his eye. "Because I do. I genuinely do. And it seems unfair I cannot please you both."

Jack covered his face. Mark knew Jack would never betray Adam and this was just serving to torment them.

Mark swiveled the chair around so he was crouching between Jack's knees. When Jack lowered his hands, Mark rested his arms on Jack's legs. They had so much history behind them, years of cohabitating, sharing everything but physical intimacy; Mark had always imagined Jack was his brother. Unfortunately, Jack didn't have the same ideals.

With the tears beginning to roll down his cheeks once more, Mark yearned for forgiveness. He let so many people down continuously he began to crave forgiveness like air. Tenderly, Jack brushed the tears from Mark's face with his thumbs while he held Mark's jaw.

"It was a mistake." Mark leaned closer to Jack's lips. "A mistake to never allow you into my bed back then. But you know why."

"Your dad." Jack dabbed at the fresh tears as they fell from Mark's eyes.

"Yes. He and Mum made me into the shambles I am. Years of counseling did nothing for me, Jackie. I've tried everything. Prozac, recreational drugs, alcohol…nothing has helped."

"Why do you feel you need to change?"

"Because. Look at what I do to those I love." Mark wanted to kiss him. He was in agony. The tiny pecks and teasing touches they had exchanged for the last two decades amounted to nothing sexually substantial. "And even now, I want to do it, to be that way with you, but there are Adam and Steve to consider."

"Yes." Jack nodded as if emphasizing it.

The worst part for Mark was his lies. He'd had sex with Keith and Carl. Jack knew he did. Why did he keep denying it? *I'm a liar and a fraud.* But Jack would not forgive him for it. Ironically, Steve had.

"I can't live with you hating me. You and Steve are all I have in this world who love me." Mark's voice broke.

"Leslie loves you."

Mark cringed at the mention of his mother, shaking his head. "No. You're very wrong there, Jack. She's ice cold. Even the thought of embracing me sickened her."

"No. I can't believe that."

"It's true." Mark's knees began to ache so he sat back on his heels. "You recall I told you about my thirteenth birthday?"

Jack tilted his head curiously.

"Remember?" Mark urged. "When my dad sent that maid to my room to deflower me?"

"Oh. Yes. I remember." Jack's mouth grew grim.

"When Mum found out, she never touched me again. I felt I was dipped in shite the way she shunned me. And for what? I was innocent. I didn't even want that woman to do it to me."

"All right," Jack whispered. "Calm down."

"It was one of Dad's filthy whores. He fucked all the help. I was thirteen. How was I to deal with him, Jack? He was such a brute to me back then." Mark wiped at his eyes roughly. "Thirteen years old and he sent that twenty-year-old woman to molest me. And the worst part was his sickening sneer after. He kept asking me if I was finally a man. I felt like throwing up."

"Shh…don't upset yourself."

"It didn't stop there. You remember? Every chance he got, he pushed those horrid women on me. In the damn horse barn, that stable girl he hired seduced me, opened my britches and sucked my damn cock. Jack, I was so young. It was warped and it fucked me up. I have no concept of how I should behave."

Jack pushed his fingers through the hair on both sides of Mark's head in an attempt to calm him.

"I can't ever tell Steven. I'm petrified he'll realize what a mental case I am. He doesn't even know how long I saw a shrink. I can't be honest with anyone but you. Jack, you're the only one who knows everything about my childhood. And if you shun me, what does that make me?" Mark rested his chin on Jack's lap. "A misfit. An outcast. That's what I feel like, love. I can't seem to fit into society. Even my looks are impossible to define. Am I a woman or am I a man?"

"You're a man. Stop torturing yourself."

"Am I? Really?" Mark scoffed. "I'm only happy when I take it up the bum. It's the only time I feel complete. A man? Me? You've got to be kidding. I'm emotional. I cry at the drop of a hat. I'm vain. I worry about my wardrobe, I get manicures! A man? Are you having a laugh?"

"Stop." Jack embraced him and squeezed him to his chest. "Stop working yourself into a state of panic."

He closed his eyes, inhaling Jack's familiar scent. Mark felt like a child in his arms.

"You are a man, Mark. You're big, athletic and masculine."

Mark choked at the last adjective.

"Yes, masculine." Jack nestled against him. "You are very attractive, that's your only crime."

"My crime. If you only knew the list of my deviances." Mark shivered in fear. "And when I lose my looks, Jack? What then? This shallow shell of a human will blow his brains out."

Jack gripped him by his shoulders and jerked him back to get a look at his face. "Shut up."

Mark blinked at the anger.

"Don't ever joke about killing yourself. You got that?"

"I'm not joking." Mark held back a sob.

"Yes, you are!" Jack shook him.

"I know you're busy—" Mark made a move to stand.

Jack kept his grip strong. "Look at me."

Suddenly shy to his gaze, Mark did with an effort.

"Though you constantly degrade yourself, you are loved. Don't ever speak of harming yourself again. You hear me?"

Mark wanted to kiss Jack so much it was torture. Jack Larsen was so beautiful inside and out, Mark wished he could be a bigamist and have two men behave like husbands to him. "When you avoid me, I get very dark impulses."

"I'm sorry." Jack laced his fingers through Mark's hair. "I take everything to heart. You know how much I wanted us to have a physical relationship. When I get these images of you screwing other men, I do go a little insane."

"Then take me."

"What?" Jack gasped in shock.

"Take it. Take what you've always wanted from me."

Jack shoved him away and stood, moving back from Mark as if he were on fire.

"We'll keep it to ourselves." Mark rose to his feet slowly.

Jack held up his hand to stop him. "You should go."

"Jackie…"

"Mark, I have work to do."

Mark knew he owed it to Jack. Somehow he felt as if he had to give something back to him after all the years of support and undying devotion Jack had given him.

With his practiced, seductive gait, Mark moved across the room to Jack, whose body language shouted fear. Mark drew close enough to kiss and whispered, "It's here. All you need do is ask."

"Oh, God…" Jack moaned in agony.

Mark put his finger to Jack's lips to shush him. "All you need do is ask," Mark echoed softly.

Chapter Five

Jack was burning up. Mark pecked his lips and swaggered his hips as he walked out of the room. Jack's skin broke out into a sweat. In shock he collapsed on his chair and wiped his face with both hands, running his fingers into his hair in agony.

How long had he waited for Mark to offer that? Motherfucker. Almost two decades? Why now?

Slowly slouching in the chair in what felt like exhaustion after Mark's visit, Jack remembered those college days so damn well.

The first day he met Mark on the baseball playing field, he drooled over him. That long brown ponytail flowing out from his baseball cap, his narrow waist and perfect ass. Jack had followed him around like a puppy. Not only was Mark physical perfection, he was a pro when it came to sports. Any sport. Jack recalled standing in line at their first crack at the bat. There was Mark, cool as a cucumber, waiting for the perfect pitch. One swing of the ash and the damn ball sailed out of the park. No bravado in Mark whatsoever, he had handed Jack the bat with a sweet smile and said, "Here ya go, love." That was it. No posturing, no self-praise.

Mark excelled at everything he ever did. Football? Wide receiver, MVP every year. He had a four-point-oh average and graduated with honors. The man was brilliant, athletic and gorgeous, yet hated himself to the point of suicide attempts.

Jack had seen the dark side of Mark as well. His depression.

"And you keep punishing him," Jack admonished himself. "You should know better, Larsen. Mark can't take it." Jack was hoping that with Steve's steadfast love, Mark would grow more self-esteem. He was wrong. His own love obviously still made a huge difference to Mark. Jack didn't want to keep putting Mark in the doghouse, he was just insanely jealous.

It had been bad enough in college when Mark forced them to double-date. Ironically, Mark never brought a woman back to their shared apartment to screw. Never. And the cock teasing Jack endured was torture.

But Jack knew Milt Richfield well from their weekend visits up to the mansion.

In certain situations Jack couldn't hide his attraction for Mark. Mark was aware Jack was hot for him. You can't hide an erection when you're in a bathing suit. But Mark's fear of disappointing his dad, and the cruelty that came with it, were major deterrents. Jack assumed Mark had to be straight.

Jack forced himself to sit upright in his chair, opening the button of his suit jacket.

The memory of Mark coming close to killing himself was brutal. Jack had no idea what Steve knew of his lover's past. And it was not up to him to divulge those details. It was up to Mark. The last thing Jack wanted to do was ruin what Mark and Steve had.

Jack had Adam now. No drama, no depression, suicide, vanity, just stability and devotion.

"I'm not going down that route with you, Mark." *But sex? No-strings-attached sex?* "Goddamn you. Is anything without a price when it comes to you, Richfield?"

Jack considered the idea of actually being able to strip Mark and have his way with him. That fantasy was so old it had actually grown cobwebs. He knew what Mark looked like naked, so that was a no-brainer.

"What a life I've led." Jack sighed tiredly. "Lusting after you." He rubbed his eyes. "Then you get engaged to Sharon, then you leave me for Steve," Jack muttered in anguish. "Damn you, Mark! My whole life has been devoted to you, and in the end, what? I'm in love with a great guy, you're coupled with Steve who adores you, and this? *Hi, Jack, how about some sex? Now?*"

Jack checked his watch. He had work to do, calls to return. "What the hell is it about you, babe?" he asked softly. "I can't deal with you or without you."

Mark glanced at his watch as he left the building and tried to pull himself together enough to meet with a client. He was late. As he hurried to the correct city block, he took out his mobile phone. "Yes, this is Mark Richfield. I have an appointment with Arnold Newhouse. I'm terribly sorry, but I'm running late."

"Yes. All right, Mr. Richfield. I'll let Mr. Newhouse know."

"Right. See you in a bit." Mark hung up, dropped his phone into his pocket and tried to forget the conversation with Jack. It had been so draining, Mark felt as if he needed a nap to recover.

He paused, straightening out his tie and suit jacket before approaching a sign on a door that read "Arnold Newhouse: Artists and Models for Hire". He opened it and stepped into the waiting area of a posh high-rise building with leather sofas and large potted plants.

"Mr. Richfield?" the woman who he had just spoken to on the phone greeted him. "Just go right in."

He gave the door a light rap before he opened it. "Arnold?"

"Mark. Come in."

He pushed back the door and found Mr. Newhouse getting to his feet from a chair behind his desk.

As he came around the desk, Mark extended his hand. "I'm

terribly sorry, Arnold. I got held up."

"No problem, Mark, have a seat."

Mark relaxed in the supple leather chair, opening the button of his suit jacket. "Yes. Well. Have you had a chance to read over the contract I provided?"

"I have." Arnold nudged it across the desk.

"Good. Very good. So? We have a deal?" Mark touched the paperwork to get a look at it. When Arnold held it back, Mark met his eyes.

"Almost."

"Almost?" Mark laughed softly. "Right." He released the contract and sat back in the chair. "Tell me what we need to change. More exposure in the media? Longer adverts on the television? Name it and I shall accommodate you."

"I want you to sign on with me."

Mark smiled shyly. He recalled their first meeting. Mr. Newhouse had made it very clear he not only wanted Mark as his advertising agent, he wanted Mark as a client. "Aren't I a bit long in the tooth to be a model?"

"Who put that idiotic idea in your head? Mark, you're stunning. Breathtaking."

"And thirty-seven."

"So? You aren't even close to the top age of the models I represent."

"No?" Mark was flattered.

Arnold stood, moving to a file cabinet. He fanned through a few folders and picked up an envelope. As he leaned against the corner of his desk, he slipped a photo out, handing it to Mark.

Mark took it. It was a beautiful headshot of a woman, obviously in her fifties, with long gray hair yet strikingly pretty.

"She's fifty-nine." Arnold smiled impishly. "One of our most popular models."

"She's lovely." Mark handed him back the photo.

Arnold placed the picture back into the envelope and returned it to the file. The man wasn't ugly, but he wasn't what Mark would consider attractive. He had a pencil-thin mustache, saggy pouches under his dark eyes, and a receding hairline with a slight attempt at a comb-over. Arnold wasn't a physical specimen either. Soft, lacking exercise, yet neither fat nor slender. A stomach bulge hung over his baggy gray trousers. He wore a wedding band and displayed family photos on his desk.

Mark disregarded Steve's claim that this agency was a front for prostitution. Arnold Newhouse was a good business and family man. Steve was wrong. At least Mark bloody hoped so. If he was propositioned, he'd get violent.

Once Arnold had returned to his chair, he leaned over the contract and said, "I'll sign yours if you sign mine."

Mark laughed nervously, trying not to think dreadful thoughts at the silliness of the comment. "What can I do? Seriously."

"What can you do? You mean modeling?"

"Yes. Who would want me?"

"Do you own a mirror?"

Mark felt his cheeks blush. "No. I mean, what type of clients? Cologne? Cars? What?"

"All of the above. You are perfect for print."

"Can I look over the contract and think about it?" Mark leaned forward to peek at the paperwork on the desk.

"What's to think about?"

"I already have a career, Arnold. How much time are we talking about here?"

"Come in next weekend for a photo shoot. We'll get you a nice portfolio. Then you do nothing until I get you a gig."

"And then what? What will it entail?"

"An hour, maybe two tops. Just you going out to locations

40

in LA and having your picture taken with the product. Mark, it's easy money."

"It'll have to be nights and weekends. I really shouldn't be using company time for personal appointments."

"Easily arranged. We have many models who have other full-time jobs."

"How long is the contract for?"

"Three years."

"What's your percentage?"

Arnold laughed softly. "I usually take twenty-five, but for you?" He paused before adding, "Fifteen."

"You want me that badly?" Mark felt an odd sensation in his gut and wondered if it was just the nerves from his earlier conversation with Jack.

"I do. Your looks will make us both very happy."

Tilting his head at the odd comment, Mark wished he could run it by Adam first. "And I can't decide tomorrow? It must be today?"

"Yes. I give you the contract for my advertising business, and you give me the contract for your modeling business."

"Can I at least read it over now?"

"Absolutely." He pushed a piece of paper across the wide desk.

Mark picked it up. It already had all his information typed into the boxes. He scanned it. Knowing contracts from his own business, he didn't think it held any mysteries. It was straightforward.

"Can I change one thing?"

"What's that?" Arnold leaned closer.

"One year? Can I begin with one year rather than three?"

"Yes. Okay." Arnold took the page back, corrected the terms and initialed it. He slid it back to Mark, holding up the pen.

His hand hovering over the dotted line, Mark wondered if this little act of offering himself out to be a model wasn't endorsing all the self-inflicted doubt he had over his looks being his only asset.

The battle raged in his head over the deed. He also knew that in a few years, when he aged, even the last bit of self-esteem he had would vanish with it. *May as well flaunt it whilst I have it.*

He signed the contract.

Instantly, Arnold handed Mark the one for his advertising business. As Mark looked it over, Arnold asked, "Can you come in this weekend for your shots?"

"Hm?" Mark glanced up at him. "What time?"

"Morning?"

"Yes. All right. Do I come here?"

"There's a studio close by." He handed Mark a business card. "Lorenzo Vashon does all our work. He's fantastic."

Mark took it, nodding.

"Saturday at nine?" Arnold picked up his telephone.

"Sorry? Oh. Yes. All right." Mark struggled to think if Steve had anything other than their usual workout run planned.

"Lorenzo? Arnold here. I'm sending you a model Saturday morning. Nine o'clock. Yes. Okay. That's all I need to know." He hung up. "He'll be there."

Another flutter made its way into Mark's gut. Why did every decision he made without consulting someone make him nervous?

Mark folded the advertising contract and slipped it into his inner jacket pocket. He rose up and held out his hand. "Thank you, Arnold."

"It's been a pleasure doing business with you, Mark."

"Yes. Good day." Mark wasn't certain he agreed. He just hoped the commitment he was making wasn't going to monopolize his time off with Steve.

Well, at least Arnold didn't expect his cock to be sucked for it like the late Jack Turner had done to all his clients. Mark was thankful for small miracles. Lately it seemed everything he did had terrible repercussions down the line. He only hoped this was going to be a bit of fun and nothing more. The last thing he needed was another problem in his life. He created too many of them on his own.

Once Mark was on street level in the boiling sun, he placed his sunglasses on his nose and took out his mobile phone to call Steve.

"'Bout time! Where the hell are you?"

"Just getting back to the parking garage." Mark hurried across the intersection.

"Why the hell did it take so long?"

With his luck Mark figured Sonja would call Steve and rat him out. Mark sighed. "I stopped by Jack's office."

"And?"

"Once again, the magnanimous Jack Larsen has granted me forgiveness."

"Really? He got over the fact that you had sex with someone else and not him?"

Mark located the car keys, feeling a jab in his heart at all the deceit. "No. I told him what he saw on the net and in the paper was just the shoot, full stop."

"So, you lied."

"Yes." Mark unlocked the car and started it up to get the air conditioning going, keeping the driver's door open until it blew cool air. "I'm a lying sack of shit."

"Calm down. Why do you always overdo it with the self-reproach?"

"Overdo it? Come on, Steven. We both know the truth."

"Stop it or I'll spank you."

That made Mark chuckle. "Want to have lunch? Can you escape?"

"Where? Name it."

"My favorite Mexican place?"

"Okay, but not on the patio. It's too damn hot."

"I know. I'm roasting in this monkey suit." Mark slid off the jacket and laid it on the passenger's seat. "Shall I pick you up? It's sort of on the way."

"Okay. I'll be out front."

"Be there in ten, traffic permitting."

"See ya."

Mark hung up, loosened his tie, and closed the driver's door. His nerves were shot but lunch with Steve would be tonic for his wounds. If there was one thing he could count on from Steve, it was love.

In the boiling heat Steve tried to stand in the shade of the building. He noticed Mark pulling up and hurried to the car. Once he sat down, he pointed the air vents at his face. "I hate LA's summers."

"Me too."

Steve had already removed his tie and rolled his sleeves up to his elbows. "Did you get a contract signed? Or did you just go and hound Jack?"

"No. I got a contract. It's in my jacket." Mark pointed his thumb to the backseat.

"Which one?"

"Artists and Models for Hire," Mark mumbled.

"You mean that front for prostitution."

"Stop! It is not. Will you quit teasing me?"

"I'm joking." Steve loved winding Mark up. "So? Good one?"

"Not bad. It's a few hundred thousand. Not exactly the BBC."

"They can't all be." Steve felt better with the air blowing on his face. "We should take a vacation."

"Where do you want to go?"

"Somewhere cold."

Mark laughed as he pulled into the restaurant parking lot.

"I assume you didn't tell Jack you were coming here."

"No. It didn't come up."

Once Mark parked in the overcrowded lot, they walked to the front of the restaurant together. The lobby was packed with businessmen and clutches of women in Capri pants and floral tops. After Mark and Steve stood in line the host took their names. Mark gestured to the bar.

"Booze?" Steve asked.

"No. Just water. I'm parched."

Steve followed Mark to the counter and sat on a high swivel stool.

"So," Steve asked, "what did Jack say?"

Before Mark could reply, their drinks were set down. They both took a deep swig to quench their thirsts.

"Mark?"

"Nothing much. Hell, I told him all that business on the net was just for the show."

"I know. You told me. What I want to know is why did you lie about it?"

"I couldn't do it. It just came out that way." Mark's cheeks hollowed out when he sipped his water through the straw.

Steve had the urge to run his tongue into the depressions. "I suppose it doesn't matter. Why torment the guy?"

"Exactly. I'm glad you see it my way, Steven."

Just as Steve had begun to lose his focus, the clientele's

conversations like a low hum to his ears, Mark's name was called. Steve spun around, and he and Mark approached the host through the tight crowd.

The room was white stucco with murals surrounding them of cactus and women in flaring red skirts dancing. Once they were seated at a table with a view of the main street out front and its congested traffic, Steve relaxed and finished his water, chewing on the ice cubes.

They'd been to the restaurant so often they didn't need to consult the menu. After the waiter had come and gone, Mark asked, "Do we have anything planned Saturday morning at around nine-ish?"

"Other than our run, no. Why?"

"I've got an appointment with a photographer."

A slow, wry smile found Steve's lips. "You couldn't resist."

"He made it part of the deal to sign on with Parsons."

"Sure he did." Steve tucked a strand of Mark's hair behind his ear.

"Honest."

"Do you know the meaning of that word?" Steve teased. When Mark appeared devastated, Steve grew upset he didn't take it as a joke. "I'm sorry. So? You have a photo shoot planned?"

"Yes. Forget it."

When Mark turned his green eyes away in what appeared to be shame, Steve urged his gaze back by touching Mark's angular jaw. "It was a joke. I didn't think of what happened between you and Jack when I said it. Tell me about this modeling job."

Mark's obvious upset at the mistaken comment altered instantly to a more passive expression. "I don't know about it yet. I have to take some photos and I suppose he sends them out."

"Is Adam representing you?"

"No. Arnold is. That's what he does, Steven, he represents models. I wanted to have Adam read over the contract but Arnold made it sound like it was a now-or-never deal."

"What? That's absurd."

The waiter set their food down in front of them, two large platters of enchiladas and rice. Both Steve and Mark requested drink refills simultaneously.

Steve began inhaling the food. "What the hell does the guy have to hide if he didn't want another agent to look over a contract?"

After he chewed and swallowed his food, Mark replied, "I read it over. There was nothing to it, really."

"Nude?"

"What?" Mark's eyes widened.

"Will the photo session be in the nude?"

"No. Of course not." Mark bristled with anger.

"You sure? Want me to come?" Steve took another mouthful of his enchilada. Mark was a babe in the woods as far as he was concerned.

"Steven."

"All right." Steve held up his hand. "Just don't get sweet-talked into taking off your pants."

"You think I'm a moron." Mark set his fork down on his plate and folded his arms.

"No. I don't. I just know sometimes you let the flattery get the best of you. Case in point, Keith O'Leary and Carl Bronson."

"Will you ever let me live it down?"

"Maybe." Steve smiled.

"And if I remember correctly, Officer Miller…"

"Yes?" Steve thought Mark was so adorable he wanted to

G.A. Hauser

kiss him.

"Uh, excuse me? Didn't those two actors have you going during that little fake police pat down?"

"Come on, Mark. Any guy would have been aroused getting their bodies felt up by two gorgeous men in uniform. Even a straight guy."

"True." Mark's green eyes twinkled mischievously.

"Kiss me." Steve leaned closer.

Mark did, grinning at him.

"Can't wait 'til later." Steve squirmed as his dick grew hard.

"Can we pass on the run? It's brutal out there."

"No. Can't pass. Sorry." Steve continued to eat.

"Slave driver."

"I'm planning on being a pile driver later." Steve ran his hand over Mark's thigh.

"Oh, yes…" Mark giggled as he resumed nibbling his food.

Steve leaned closer to hiss, "I want to fuck you so hard you cry for mercy."

"I'll cry for more. Not mercy."

A chill washed over Steve's hot skin. He could not wait to strip Mark and screw him again. With Mark's wicked smile aimed his way as they ate, it was like Steve kept falling in love with Mark again and again. "I love you," he whispered.

"And I love you too." Mark added after another bite of his food, "You big ole softie."

Home once again after a long afternoon of making phone calls and appointments for the never-ending commercial advertising business, Mark came through the door, kicking off his shoes and dreading the run in the heat.

Right behind him, Steve thumbed through the mail he'd

removed from their box. The door to the two-car garage connected to the kitchen, where Steve paused to drop the envelopes on the table.

Since he knew he had to get this grueling run over with, Mark went upstairs to their walk-in closet, undressed and hung up his suit. Once he was naked, he found a clean jock strap and stepped into it. Meanwhile Steve stood behind him, going through the same routine.

As Mark adjusted his anatomy to sit comfortably in his jockstrap, Steve leaned down and licked his exposed ass cheek.

"It's too hot to run. Please?" Mark begged.

"A two-mile sprint. That's it. We'll be done in less than fifteen minutes." Leaving the closet in just his briefs, Steve changed into his running shorts while standing in the bedroom.

Once he found a clean pair of shorts, Mark dragged them up his legs, groaning in agony.

Their master bedroom was twice the size of the other bedrooms in the house. Since they'd purchased the home new, Mark had it designed to his liking. The bedroom walls were taupe. Not ivory, not off white. Taupe. The artwork that hung on the walls ranged from Steve's bold lithographs of male torsos to Mark's more subtle abstracts. Though Mark had thought the combination odd at first, they did fit in well. *Like me and my Steve.* He smiled as he stared at one of the nude torsos, continuing to get ready.

"We need a pool." Steve dug a pair of socks out of his drawer, and sat on the bed to put them on.

"Jack had one at his place before he moved into Adam's house." Mark used a rubber band he kept on the nightstand to pull his hair back into a ponytail.

"So? Are you saying we should have bought Jack's old house? How weird would that have been?" Steve cocked his eyebrow at Mark.

Mark brought his focus back to his lover. "Not weird at all.

It was my home too." He sat on the bed to tug on his white socks. "Are you wearing a shirt?"

"No. It's too frickin' hot." Steve stuffed his hand down the front of his own shorts.

"Wood?" Mark asked, amused.

"I always get wood when I'm in a room with you."

After giving Steve a big sniff to inhale his scent, Mark snuggled against him. "Wouldn't you rather have a fuck marathon and burn the calories off that way?"

"We will. After the run. Ready?"

His bottom lip forming his classic Richfield little boy pout, Mark stood, took his baseball cap from the dresser, and popped it on his head. Next on the list were his sunglasses, which he stuck on his nose. "I feel naked without a shirt."

"Wear one." Steve tied his shoelaces.

"No. Not for fifteen minutes. So? Where's the two-mile marker?"

"Ten blocks out, ten back."

"Full sprint?"

"Well, ya can't sprint full out for that long. Just the last few blocks. But faster than our normal pace."

With his arms crossed over his bare chest, Mark watched Steve take one key off his chain and lace it into his running shoe. Once Steve had his sunglasses on as well, he waved for Mark to go.

Mark plodded down the carpeted stairs heavily and out the front door of their home. Though the property appeared lush and green from a sprinkler system and an expert landscaper, the illusion of a tropical oasis was soon exchanged for the suffocating dry heat when they left the air-conditioned house.

"Let's get this over with." Steve took off.

Mark raced after him, already overheated. "Christ! This fast?"

"Yes. Otherwise we can run our usual four miles."

"No. No, this is fine." Mark cringed at the frantic pace. While he ran he looked into the passing cars. A myriad of wealth was on display from their high-class neighbors. Porsches, Mercedes and BMWs cruised by, all taking a peek at them as they worked out.

Mark asked, "I wonder if they think we're completely mad?"

"Mad dogs and Englishmen."

"Yes. Quite. So, are you the mad dog then?"

"Funny." Steve stepped up the speed.

"Augh! You really want this to be punishing?" Mark knew in a pinch he could run faster than Steve. He just didn't know for how long.

"Yes. Punish me." Steve laughed.

"Fine!" Mark flew past him.

Mark had a feeling Steve was struggling to keep up, hearing his rasping breaths behind him. He wasn't prepared when Steve shouted, "Ten blocks! About face."

Thrown off pace, screeching to a halt, Mark spun around and found Steve had used the stop as an advantage to gain some ground. Mark dug deep for the energy to catch up.

By the time they were closing in on the front door, it was an all-out dash to be first. Mark didn't let up this time to allow Steve his slap at the front door. Instead, he gnashed his teeth and pushed past his pain to get there before Steve did.

They ended up slamming shoulders right up the white stone pathway to the door. Mark reached out and punched the door first, buckling over and gasping for air.

Obviously in agony, Steve retreated from the front stoop and dropped to his back on the finely trimmed grass, knees bent, moaning.

"Give me that fucking key." Mark trapped Steve's running

51

shoe and untied it. The heat making him dizzy, he entered the house, threw his cap and sunglasses on the living room's cream leather sectional sofa, and turned the thermostat down a degree. Immediately he tugged the band out of his hair, and then he stuck his head under the cold running tap in the kitchen sink to stop from getting heatstroke and keeling over.

As the water cooled his head, Mark let out a long low whimper from the relief until he felt something ice cold on his ass. He spun around, spraying water all over the kitchen from his soaked hair.

Right behind him, Steve held a tray of ice cubes and had slipped one into the back of Mark's gym shorts.

"Running in this heat can't be healthy." Mark wiped the water off his face and leaned back against the stainless steel double-basin sink.

Steve placed the ice cube tray aside and handed Mark a bottle of water. Mark took it and almost choked, he was guzzling it so quickly.

His own bottle of water consumed and disposed of, Steve again went back to the tray of ice. With a cube in each hand, he smoothed them around Mark's pectoral muscles and abs.

The sweat still pouring from his body, Mark closed his eyes in relief.

Steve dug into the front of Mark's shorts and jock strap. A fast-melting cube was pressed against Mark's soft dick. He flinched but didn't refuse the gesture.

"Nice?" Steve asked seductively.

"I'm hot."

"I'll say."

"We really should not be running in one-hundred-degree heat, love."

"No. You're probably right." Steve removed another ice cube out of the tray and stuck it down Mark's shorts.

The frozen cube slid against his boiling crotch. At the first touch of the frigid temperature, Mark jumped, relaxing as it cooled his boiling body off.

Steve dragged Mark's shorts down his thighs, exposing his cock from the athletic supporter. He slid the dripping cube over Mark's erection. As the chilly sensation ran under the base of his corona, Mark shivered visibly. Steve removed another fresh cube and smoothed it up and down Mark's engorged dick. It felt so tantalizing, Mark leaned all his weight against the counter and spread his legs as far as he could within the confines of the lowered clothing.

"Feel good?" Steve asked, dropping Mark's shorts down to the floor.

"Hm hmm." Mark stepped out of them so he could spread his legs wider.

Steve cupped another ice cube against Mark's balls. The melting water raced down his inner thighs to his knees. Steve ran one cube over Mark's testicles to his ass and the other up and down his cock.

No one had ever done this to Mark before. He was enthralled with the new sensation. The kitchen floor was becoming a puddle as the ice quickly turned to water and ran down Mark's legs.

"Bloody fantastic," Mark crooned.

When one of the cubes was small, Steve popped it into his mouth and kissed Mark, blowing the tiny chunk of ice into his mouth. It melted instantly on Mark's tongue.

Steve simulated fucking Mark's mouth. After that deep sensuous kiss, Steve stepped backwards to place a gap between them.

A feeling of euphoria began to wash over Mark at the exotic foreplay. He gazed down to see his jock strap off kilter and his glistening wet dick and balls exposed, protruding from the ribbons of elastic material like an obscene photo spread in a gay magazine.

Being shy by nature, he lowered his hands to shield the view.

"Don't." Steve pushed his hands away. "Let me admire you."

His cheeks burning with his growing sexual need and the pleasure the teasing gave his lover, Mark opened his arms wide, showing off his body with more pride. His large endowment excited Steve and he enjoyed giving Steve what he loved.

When a shiver washed down his spine, Mark wondered if this was what it would feel like to be photographed again. Years ago, in his youth, a woman took a few risqué shots of him for a coffee table book of male nudes. None exposed his genitals.

"Steve." Mark wanted them to make love. Now.

As if shaking himself from a trance, Steve reached out for Mark's cock and tugged on it. Mark could only grow more amused. His lover used his prick like a leash and led him to the bedroom.

Once they ascended the stairs and were beside the bed, Steve stripped off all his own clothing and found the lube.

When Mark attempted to remove the jock strap, Steve scolded him. "Hey, don't touch that."

Mark stopped what he was doing, allowing Steve to play.

With a hand on each of Mark's shoulders, Steve placed him in front of a full-length mirror inside their walk-in closet. From behind, Steve urged Mark to bend over.

Once he took a look at their reflections, Mark could tell by Steve's expression he was in the zone. The ultimate sex zone he sometimes fell into during their lovemaking. Steve's cock filled Mark from behind. After the initial contact and penetration, Mark opened his eyes again, looking in the mirror. Steve was focusing on Mark's constricted balls and cock, still in the same tangle of jockstrap elastic, engorged and blushing red. It felt both uncomfortable and arousing to be trapped that way.

Steve's gaze flittered between Mark's face and his cock. He appeared to be on another planet.

Mark reached for the wall beside the mirror to brace himself. Steve's thrusts became deeper and quicker. Soon Steve's heavy breathing and grunting filled the small space. Mark felt his own cock grow even thicker as it waited its turn for release. With Steve going wild behind him, Mark's dick was completely erect and stiff at the thrill of being ridden by his lover.

"Mark," Steve moaned. "Oh, Mark…"

"Yes. Come for me, baby." Mark whimpered in yearning.

"Ah, Mark!"

At the depth of penetration and the throbbing of Steve's cock up his ass, Mark shivered in pleasure, and his dick began to drip pre-come from the rush. Steve's grip was like a vise on Mark's hips. He ground in for the last few waves of orgasm. Both of them gasping again, just like after their sprint, Mark waited. Steve seemed to be savoring being inside him. Mark hated it when he pulled out.

Inevitably, they separated. Steve stumbled back as if he were dizzy from the climax. Mark turned to look over his shoulder at Steve, who headed to the bathroom to wash up.

Still trying to catch his breath, Mark straightened his back and looked at himself in the mirror. He was obscene. His dick was so big it appeared an out-of-proportion appendage to his slender form.

Before he had time to consider anything else, Steve had spun him around. On his knees before Mark, Steve grabbed Mark's dick in both hands and plunged it into his mouth.

"Yes! Oh, lover, yes." Mark's legs grew shaky and he reached out for something to keep him upright. While he gripped the rod where their clothing hung, his cock was devoured by a sex fiend.

His balls still wrapped up in a sadomasochistic-like

contraption, Mark yearned to tug off the elastic and set them free. But he knew Steve wanted it this way. Steve's fingers rolled over the skin of Mark's protruding testicles as he sucked like a Hoover.

Even as the pleasure shot through him, Mark imagined if he released his grip on the bar he'd collapse. Between the long emotional day, the run, the heat and getting it up the ass, he was exhausted.

Just when he was about to cry uncle and give up on being able to come, Steve stripped the confining jock strap down to Mark's ankles and shoved two fingers up his ass. Mark shouted out in surprise and shivered with an orgasm. His moans echoed in the small space of the closet. Steve milked Mark's cock dry and massaged his prostrate deeply.

Unable to hold himself up any longer, Mark cried, "Babe...babe..." in jerking breaths. The minute his dick was free of Steve's mouth, Mark dropped to his knees with fatigue.

Steve grabbed Mark's jaw, his eyes on fire. "You fantastic motherfucker! I love you! I love you!"

As Steve covered his face with kisses, Mark moaned, "It was brilliant, love and you're welcome."

Chapter Six

Saturday morning Mark drove his dark blue European sports car, his beloved TVR, into the city and found ample street parking. He wore a pair of his favorite threadbare jeans, a black tank top and flip-flops. He could already feel the summer's boiling heat at nine in the morning.

While making his way down the block, Mark checked the business card again and located a small photography shop among the plethora of retail establishments. He tried the door. It was locked.

He shielded the glare and leaned against the glass to see a darkened room. No one was in sight, so he removed his mobile phone from his pocket. Just as he began to dial the number on the card, he noticed a man rushing from a back room to the door.

"Hello. Sorry. I was getting the studio ready."

"It's all right." Mark stepped inside the dim, musty interior. A front lobby area was plastered with large framed landscape photographs and runway models. He assumed they were Lorenzo's originals. A small L-shaped dark blue sofa, coffee table strewn with magazines and a palm tree in a terra cotta pot in the corner made up the contents of the front room.

"Come. Come inside."

As the man relocked the front door, Mark inspected him.

Though Lorenzo wasn't tall, he was very attractive. Solid, muscular, jet black hair and designer stubble, white cotton pants and T-shirt, and bare feet.

He showed him to the back room. They were alone. No assistants, no prying eyes.

Mark pushed his sunglasses to the top of his head and examined this second room. It was painted white. Newspapers held by masking tape covered the windows, and one wall had someone's headshots pinned to it over a table that acted as a desk. It was slightly rough, not what he'd expected, and it too had a peculiar smell he could not readily identify. He wondered if the odors were from the restaurant next door.

Lorenzo stopped rushing around and spun to look at Mark. "Right. What have we here?"

Mark rested his hands on his hips and waited for Lorenzo's appraisal.

"Yes…very nice. Sit. Sit." He gestured to a stool in front of a white-sheet backdrop.

Mark sat down.

Lorenzo removed the sunglasses from Mark's hair, setting them aside on top of a mound of paperwork on a tiny desk. With both hands he fluffed Mark's tresses up, fussing with the fringe that covered his forehead and eyebrows.

After the primping, Lorenzo backed up to his camera, which rested on a high tripod. He leaned down and looked through the lens. "Look at the wall to your left."

The shutter whirred and clicked.

As Lorenzo spoke them, Mark obeyed the directions quietly, remembering his first experience modeling in front of the camera. The photographer, Janis Campbell, had spotted him when he had a part in an underground all-male production of *My Fair Lady*. How he had ever gotten talked into playing Eliza Doolittle was anyone's guess. Stripped naked on stage, his character placed into a bathtub for a wash by the maids—or in this version, butlers—Mark was revealed to the world. Though the timing had been rehearsed, and the lights were supposed to go out as his trousers dropped and he covered his crotch, the timing was off. He had been exposed to a packed theater; over two hundred people, including his mother, had seen his dick. Mark thought back on that play and cringed, still feeling sick to his stomach about it.

"What happened?" Lorenzo stood up from his camera. "Why did you make that face?"

"Sorry." Mark tried to keep his expression under control.

"Stand up."

Lorenzo approached him as if to speak confidentially. "Listen, my friend…"

Instinctively, Mark leaned down to hear him.

"You have a very feminine quality to you. Perhaps your face."

Mark winced. *Here we go. Time for the slap to my ego.*

"Would you be averse to removing your shirt so I may take shots showing your chest? To reinforce the man in you."

Without a word, Mark pulled his shirt over his head, his mouth forming a bitter line at the all-too-familiar conclusion.

"Good." Lorenzo walked back to his camera.

Again, listening to his instructions, Mark tossed his T-shirt down on the floor and stood tall.

Memories washed over him with vengeance. The infamous Janis Campbell. How was he to know she was one of the leading photographers of male nudes? Her hardbound coffee-table book, *American Male-Men*, sold four million copies, and he was in that book. He'd never heard of her. At twenty-one, he'd been eager to please. Painfully naïve, he rarely used the word *no*. The yearning in him to be accepted by his peers, be seen as worthy and appealing was even more of a burden back then, until he'd met the reliable Jack Larsen.

Though he had no exhibitionist tendencies, Mark had stripped naked for Janis. All the other men in the room were naked too, so he couldn't very well cry modesty after agreeing to pose for her.

Those other men strutted around like proud peacocks. Hard-ons were everywhere he looked.

Finally when his opportunity arrived, Mark posed for this young female prodigy. Janis took one picture of him naked in a shower; another in bed, the sheet pulled down to his pubic hair; yet another, lying on the back of a fantastic white stallion. Dedra Dunn. He remembered the horse's name. He begged his father to buy the horse for him. They already had three thoroughbreds, what was one more Arabian? Mark's mother gave in to his pleading. Leslie knew if Mark loved that horse, he'd be at their estate every weekend to ride. And he was.

"Good." Lorenzo approached him again. He fussed with Mark's hair, creating a chill up his spine. "Sit down on the cushions."

Mark turned to where he pointed, noticing the floor was covered with pillows. As he sat down, Lorenzo moved the high stool out of the way.

"Relax. Stretch out your long legs." Lorenzo removed Mark's flip-flops, and gave him a long, intense stare. Mark held his breath as Lorenzo reached down and opened the top button of Mark's blue jeans.

Without a word, Lorenzo headed back to his camera.

It was warm in the room and began to take on the distinct odor of curry or some other spicy cooking. The air conditioning might have been on, but it wasn't what Mark would call cool and the smell was unappetizing first thing in the morning.

He had considered wearing shorts but didn't think it would be appropriate. In reality, he'd expected to be given something formal to wear. He had no idea he'd be photographed in his casual attire, or worse, without it.

Propped up on one elbow as he lay on his side, Mark stared at the camera lens, his best friend and worst enemy. He imagined he was so vain he'd become a Botox queen, or perhaps get a nip-tuck in his mid-forties. It seemed to work for everyone in Hollywood. Why not him?

Lorenzo positioned Mark's free hand to rest right next to the bulge in his crotch before he moved back and clicked the shutter of his camera.

As Lorenzo reloaded his camera with another roll of film, Mark asked, "You don't use a digital camera?"

"No."

After pondering the curt answer, Mark added, "This is for my portfolio, right?"

"Yes."

With the heat of his own hand warming his inner thigh, Mark took a good look at his pose. "It seems slightly seductive."

"It is. Don't you know sex sells, my friend?"

Mark smiled wryly. He was in advertising and certainly recognized that old adage.

Once he loaded his film, Lorenzo looked back at him. "You're very sexual. The type of clients who will want you will be for sexy type ads. You'll see." He took several shots then took a step closer and instructed, "Lie against the pillows and face me."

Mark repositioned himself so his back was almost upright on the high mountain of cushions. Without using verbal commands, Lorenzo nudged his knees apart in a wide straddle, opening his body for the camera. Next he arranged his arms to rest on top of the foam cushions. The posture would be overtly lewd if Mark were naked.

In a dark place in his mind, Mark expected Lorenzo to ask him to take off his pants. The session began to take on a personal feel, as if Lorenzo were fulfilling a private passion of his own.

"Relax your straddle. You're a man, not a woman."

Kicked in the groin again, Mark snarled involuntarily and allowed his legs to splay open.

"Better."

"What fucking client will want shots like this?"

"All of them."

Suspicion reared its ugly head. "How many more do you have to take?"

As if he were insulted, Lorenzo straightened up behind his tripod. "What do you care? You're not paying for them."

Fed up, Mark made a move to stand.

"Fine. Be a baby. I hope when Arnold sends you to clients you don't pout and have a tantrum."

The insult cut deep. Mark dropped back to his rump again on the cushions.

"Who's in this business? Me or you?"

Mark glared at him. "We both are. I sell advertising."

"Sell? You sell advertising and you think you know about photography and art?" Lorenzo knelt down next to him. "You have a strong sexual aura. Why does it bother you to share it with the camera?"

"I just started feeling used." Mark felt that stupid lump in his throat again. What the hell was he, three years old?

"You will be used." Lorenzo stroked Mark's hair back from his face. "Your photo will be used to sell products. Your image will entice those who look at it to purchase goods. Isn't this what modeling is about? Selling yourself? Selling with your body and your face?"

In humiliation, Mark lowered his lashes. "Yes."

"If I looked like you, I'd use it to get everything I needed. Don't be selfish with your beauty."

Mark met his dark eyes. The intensity of the stare made the gooseflesh rise on his arms.

"When you go to your appointments, raise your head high. Do you know how many men and women out there would love to be in your shoes? Would die to have their looks photographed to make money?" Lorenzo used two fingers to hold Mark's chin in his hand.

Not liking the touch, Mark moved his face out of Lorenzo's grasp. "All right. I get it. What next?"

After a pause, Lorenzo asked, "I wonder if you would be averse to removing your jeans?"

Mark knew he had nothing under them, and growled, "No."

"I'm only joking." Lorenzo laughed as he walked back to his camera.

Finally released from his session, Mark held his phone to his ear and paused outside the studio in the glare of the sun. "Hey, love."

"Hi, babe. How did the shoot go?"

Once he placed his sunglasses on, Mark crossed the street, which had gotten busier since he parked before nine this morning. "All right. Sort of what I expected."

"Did he ask you to take off your clothing?"

"Yes, but he immediately said he was joking after." Mark used the key fob to unlock his car door. "Christ, it's hot. My car is boiling." He opened the door and climbed in, starting it to get the cool air blowing.

"Adam invited us to his place for a day at the beach."

"Oh?" Mark closed the car door and fastened his seatbelt. "With Jack?"

"I assume so. He does live there."

"I'm game. Are you?"

"We should do wind sprints on the sand."

"Steven, is everything a workout to you?" Mark signaled and placed the car in drive, pulling out of the parallel parking spot.

"I just feel weird when I don't do it."

"You are weird." Mark paused at a traffic light. "We should bring something. Tell me what to pick up on my way home."

"Beer. Condoms. Lube."

Mark cracked up. "I love placing those three items on a conveyer belt."

"Good. See you soon."

"Later." Mark hung up, shaking his head at his shopping list.

The grocery bag in his arms, Mark entered the house, listening for signs of life as he stepped into the living room. "Love?"

"I'm here."

After he set the bag on the kitchen table, he spun around. Steve was posing seductively against the doorframe in his black Speedos.

"Nice."

"Come here, gorgeous." Steve hugged Mark close for a kiss. Mark moaned at the passionate smooching. "You're revving my engines up." Steve squirmed all over him.

"What time do Jack and Adam expect us?"

Steve raised Mark's tank top and lapped his tongue all over his chest. "Later."

"Should I put the beer in the fridge?"

"Later." Steve popped open his jeans, reaching his hand inside them. "I am so glad you never wear briefs."

"Not never." Mark laughed softly.

Steve peeled the tight jeans down Mark's legs. When his ass was bare, Steve urged him to lie over the kitchen table. While Mark rested his head on his arms, the grocery bag rustled.

A moment later, Steve's slick cock was inside him.

"Ah, yes. Perfect, love." Mark hummed happily.

They had made love in every room of the house. Mark had always heard gay men thought about sex every nine seconds. He was convinced with Steve it was every three.

The table creaked and moaned as Steve hammered into his body. With the tips of his fingers, Mark reached for the edge of the table's wooden top, holding on to keep it from shifting across the tile floor.

"Baby, baby, baby…" Steve crooned in delirium. "I love your ass! Christ, it's so tight."

Mark flexed his muscles, making it even tighter. "How about now?" he teased.

Steve howled in delight. "I don't wanna come, I wanna fuck you all day."

"Fuck me all day."

"I have to come. I have to."

Mark laughed at Steve's dilemma, then rested his cheek on the cool lacquered surface of the table, closing his eyes. He loved it when Steve was inside him. *Loved it.*

"You. Sexy. Mother. Fucker." With each word, Steve thrust his hips deeply.

"Mm," Mark replied.

A last, violent plunge, shifting the kitchen table a foot across the floor, and Steve came. Mark savored the hot throbbing inside his bottom. "Oh, yes. What a welcome home. I do love it."

Steve collapsed against Mark's back, gasping.

"Good one?"

"It's always a good one with you, Richfield."

G.A. Hauser

Once Steve disconnected, Mark turned around to look at him. His sheathed cock, poking out of his black swimsuit, was still hard. The reserved tip was filled with white cream.

Mark tugged a paper towel off the dispenser and removed the rubber for him.

"Thanks, babe." Steve used some damp paper towels to clean up, asking, "You want me to suck you?"

"I'm good for now." Mark washed his hands.

"Go change. I'll get the towels and sunblock."

"Okay." Mark's jeans still low around his hips, Steve gave his tush a good-natured slap as he passed.

Chapter Seven

Through the classic traffic of LA, Mark drove them to Adam and Jack's beachfront home in Malibu. The streets and highways were jammed with locals and tourists alike, playing in their posh designer outfits and limousines. Chihuahuas' tongues wagged from their perches in Gucci purses as the elite made a grand showing of their latest accessories.

It was baking hot and there was little shade. Mark parked in Adam's driveway, as close to a swaying palm tree as he could get, then shut off the car and reached behind the seat for the beer while Steve grabbed their canvas bag with the beach items in it.

"I love Adam's house." Steve closed the car door behind him, admiring the façade.

"Me too. It's what everyone envisions when they think of a Southern California home." Before Steve knocked on the door, Mark reminded him, "Nothing about the sex with Keith and Carl. Got it?"

"Got it." Steve kissed Mark's nose.

When the door swung back, Adam opened it wide to invite them in. "Hello, boys."

"Hiya, Adam." Steve gave him a warm hug. "Where's He-man?"

"On the back deck." Adam took the beer from Mark.

"Thanks, sweetie."

"My pleasure." Mark pecked his cheek.

They passed through the cool, breezy rooms decorated in a southwestern décor. Hand-woven Mexican tapestries hung on the walls and white ceramic tiles covered the floors. Ceiling fans spun, the air creating pleasant drafts.

Adam asked, "Beer or margarita?"

"Margarita," Steve replied enthusiastically. "You do make the best ones around."

Mark smiled at Adam, nodding. "Yes, please." He continued to pass through the house to the back sliding doors as Adam and Steve engaged in a conversation in the kitchen.

Once he shifted the door back, Mark found Jack in his swimsuit sitting on a lounge chair, an empty margarita glass on the sandy patio under him. When Mark stepped out, Jack turned to look.

"Hello, Jackie."

"Hi, Mark."

Mark leaned close and pecked Jack's cheek, wanting to sit on his lap and snuggle.

"Steve inside?"

It felt like strained small talk and Mark could hardly bear it. "Yes, watching Adam mix his magical potion."

Jack's gaze returned to the action on the beach and the curling waves.

Mark slid a chair close to sit next to him. "You okay, Jackie?"

"I'm fine, Mark."

"Thanks for inviting us over."

"No problem."

After taking a quick look behind him into the kitchen, Mark placed his hand on Jack's enormous bare quadriceps. Instantly Jack whipped his head around to face him. "Have you given any thought to my offer?"

"Yes. Too much." Jack brushed Mark's hand off his leg.

Before Mark could go any further in the conversation, Adam and Steve stepped out onto the patio. Mark took the glass Steve handed him. "Thanks."

As the men scooted over two more chairs, Steve asked, "Mark, what was the name of that cover for the prostitution studio called?"

Mark chided, "It's not a prostitution ring."

Adam sipped his drink. "What's the name of it, Mark?"

Before he replied, Mark peered at Jack, who was staring at him through his Ray-Bans. "Artist and Models for Hire."

"Never heard of them."

"Surprise, surprise," Steve groaned, gulping the green liquid in his glass.

"Who owns it?" Adam moved his chair so he could rest his feet on Jack's shins.

Mark wished he could use Jack as a hassock as well. "Arnold Newhouse."

"Never heard of him either. Did you check him out on the web before you signed?"

"No." Mark could feel Jack's eyes on him. Glaring? Calling him stupid and a fool? What?

Steve gestured with an open hand as if showing the other two how impulsive Mark was. "The guy wouldn't let him read the contract, Adam. How lame is that?"

"Mark?" Adam tried to get his attention.

"What."

"What's the deal?"

Mark moved his gaze out to the rough tide and bobbing bodies cooling off in the heat. He shrugged in reply. He knew damn well the modeling deal was vain and it was embarrassing in its cry for attention.

"He had his session with a photographer this morning," Steve informed the other two men, setting his empty glass on the cement patio.

"Nude?" Jack sneered.

"No." Mark pouted at him. "Jackie…be nice."

"Topless?" Jack pursued.

While the other three waited for his answer, Mark balanced his glass on the patio, stood and walked past them to the beach. He knew they'd talk about him after he left. He hated it but he couldn't take constantly defending his actions to everyone around him as if he were a child.

The hot wind whipping his hair around his face, he continued down the white sand to the dampness of the tide. When the beach grew wet, he took off his flip-flops, dug his toes into the cool sand and gazed off at the horizon.

No matter how old he was, he always felt like a stupid kid. His decisions were placed under a microscope and analyzed to death, his actions judged, his life constantly scrutinized.

Once he stepped back onto the dry sand, Mark set his sandals down, took off his gym shorts and top, revealing his Speedos, and dropped his sunglasses on the pile. Then, moving in a straight line, he speared through a wave and swam out a few yards into the choppy ocean.

When he found his footing after a large set of waves, he turned back to look at the house. The three men were still sitting on the patio. What did he expect? Someone would join him? They needed to criticize his decisions. Commiserate together over having to deal with someone like him in their lives.

He floated over another wave, distracted by the body-boarders and distant surfers who were beyond the jetty.

Someone bumped into him from behind.

"Oops! Sorry, miss."

When Mark turned around to see the older man, the man's face expressed his surprise. "Miss?" Mark sneered.

70

"Sorry." The man swam away quickly.

At the insult, Mark closed his eyes tiredly. He knew he needed to trim his hair. Steve and Jack had conservative cuts. Ironically, Adam's was down to his shoulders. Mark wondered if that was a request from Jack, for Adam to grow his hair as long as Mark's. It did seem a bit odd.

But Mark liked his hair long. As he touched its length, he felt very attached to his shaggy locks. He knew damn well they were a big part of what made him attractive. "And feminine," he muttered out loud.

"Won't anyone come out and play?" Mark wanted someone to miss him. Join him.

Adam went inside again. Mark assumed it was to refill the margaritas. Steve stood, shielding his eyes from the sun as he searched the water. Mark wondered whether Steve or Jack could see him. Just in case, he waved. "Come out, baby," Mark coaxed quietly.

A small boat pulled up near him. "Excuse me."

Mark spun around to see two buff lifeguards in the craft. "Yes?"

"You're drifting too far from shore. Could you swim in?"

"Oh. Sorry."

"No problem." The man winked flirtatiously at him.

Mark assumed the lifeguard knew he was a man and not a woman.

With a few strong strokes of the front crawl, Mark swam to the cresting waves again. When he found his feet, he looked back at the house. Only Adam and Jack were sitting on the deck.

Just as he was about to head out, someone grabbed him around his waist. He gasped and looked over his shoulder. The moment he realized it was Steve, Mark sighed in relief.

"Hey."

"Hey. You gave me a fright."

Steve released Mark so he could face him. "Did you think I was a shark?"

"You are a shark." Mark wrapped his arms around Steve's neck.

"What did that lifeguard say to you? Did he try to pick you up?"

"No. He told me to swim in. I was too far out."

"Oh." Steve held Mark's waist, riding over the waves with him.

"Are the others joining us?"

"I doubt it."

"What did you discuss when I left?"

"You."

"I figured." Mark glanced back at the shore.

"We just worry about you, Richfield."

"Don't. I'm a big boy."

"I'll say." Steve cupped the front of Mark's bathing suit.

"Do you always have a one-track mind?"

"Yes. You. Unless you want me to have two tracks. Your ass and your cock."

"Funny." Mark narrowed his eyes at him.

"Ever fuck in the ocean?"

"No. There are children around. Behave."

"Just asking."

"Do you like children?" Mark asked.

"Hm? Me? Like children?"

"Yes."

"I suppose. I don't want any though."

"No?"

"No." Steve waited until they floated over another wave

before he said, "Please don't tell me you do."

"I suppose it's one motivation for marrying a woman."

"Maark," Steve moaned. "You drive me insane! What are you going to do now? Find a goddamn breeder? Knock up a woman so you can have offspring?"

The comments mortified him. Was this what Steve really thought of him? "Let go!" Mark shoved at Steve's hands, which were grasping his hips.

"Why? Where are you going?"

"Steven!" Mark attempted to shrug off his hold but Steve was extremely powerful and determined when he wanted to be.

"You're not going anywhere."

"You say the most insulting things." Mark struggled to push him back when another large wave elevated them off their feet.

"Me?" In a sarcastic voice, Steve mimicked, "I suppose it's one motivation for marrying a woman."

"Shut up. Let go." Steve's fingers had grasped Mark's swimsuit in an effort to keep him still. Mark wrenched Steve's hand to get him to release it. "You're pulling me bloody bathing suit off, ya wanker!"

"I love it when you get mad. You get all British on me."

In an attempt to stay clothed, gripping the front of his suit with both hands, Mark began wading in. Steve was attached to the waistband and as they proceeded to the shore, the back of Mark's bathing suit stayed behind.

"Let go," Mark snarled, twisting.

Steve teased, "Keep pulling and it'll rip off."

"Steve!" Mark wasn't playing. He was infuriated. He could see his shirt and sunglasses not far off. He tried to pry Steve's fingers from his Speedo.

Steve tripped on the undercurrent, dropping the back of Mark's swimsuit to his mid-thighs. Mark was horrified to have

G.A. Hauser

his backside exposed. Of course, to Steve it was hilarious. Mark finally escaped from his grasp and hurried to his belongings.

In a huff, Mark gathered up his shirt, shorts, flip-flops and sunglasses. He held his suit up, thinking it was so stretched out it would fall to his knees if he released it, and stormed to the house.

Jack and Adam watched his approach.

Behind him, Steve was chasing after him, unable to contain his laughter. "Mark. Wait. Come on."

"Get away from me." Mark ground his jaw.

"It was a joke. I was having some fun."

"What now?" Adam asked as Mark drew near.

Before he entered the house to change, Mark spun around and pointed an accusing finger at Steve. "He thinks it's amusing to humiliate me in public."

"Mark…lighten up." Steve caught his breath and put his hands on his hips.

"Lighten up?" Mark growled, his teeth clenched so tight he was about to explode. "You exposed me out there. Do you think that's funny?"

"It was, a little." Steve gave him a boyish smile.

"I fail to see the humor." Mark turned back to the sliding door.

"Then don't talk to me about wanting kids." Steve's jovial voice changed drastically in tone.

"Oh, no." Adam rubbed his face tiredly.

"Is nothing private between us?" Mark accused his lover.

"Come on, Mark," Steve admonished. "I need help when it comes to dealing with you."

"Oh, that's it." Mark brushed the sand from his feet, threw back the sliding door and entered the house, intent on changing and leaving.

He was so angry he was seething. He stood in the bathroom

74

on the first level of the house and threw his things onto the tile floor, taking a moment to calm down before he changed out of his wet suit.

A soft knock sounded on the door. "Go away, Steven."

"It's not Steve. It's me."

Shocked it was Jack, Mark opened the door.

"Are you all right?" Jack asked softly.

"No. I'm bloody not."

Jack entered the small room, closing the door behind him. "What happened?"

"I made one insignificant comment about how having children was one reason to marry a woman, and the dumb cop assumed I'd locate a breeder and fornicate."

"You can be impulsive that way."

"Jack! Don't side with him."

"Come here, baby."

At the amazing offer, Mark melted and embraced him. Swept up in memories of Jack's strength being his salvation for almost two decades, Mark turned to putty in his grasp. The large solidness of Jack's upper body was foreign now. Mark was used to holding Steve. Though Steve was fit, he wasn't as enormous as this brawny blond. When you hugged Jack Larsen you felt dwarfed by his size.

It had always made Mark feel more like a woman. Maybe that was what he feared from Jack, becoming a woman in his embrace.

Jack's lips brushed Mark's neck. The tingle it sent through Mark, the memories of Jack's kindness, his care, his attention, brought him to the verge of tears once more. Life was so unfair. Why couldn't he love two men? Why? Have them both live in his home, have them both use his body for sex? Why not?

"You feel better now?" Jack stepped back to see his face.

"Oh, Jackie…" Mark bit his lip as it quivered.

"Please don't cry."

"I miss you."

"There's nothing to miss. I'm here."

"No. I mean living with you. Having you to talk to, to share our days." Mark wanted to feel Jack inside him. He'd never had the pleasure and now he craved it. When he and Jack were roommates, he'd never imagined anal sex would be so fulfilling. He wished he had known then what he knew now. With his one hand cupping Jack's square jaw, he whispered sensuously, "Jackie-blue."

Jack gave Mark a feather-light peck on his lips. It was so exciting, it made Mark's toes curl.

"I have to get back to Adam. I just wanted to make sure you were all right."

Mark found Jack's hand and urged it downwards. As he stared into Jack's turquoise eyes, Mark slid Jack's hand inside his damp bathing suit to his erection.

"No. We can't do this, Mark."

With Jack's hand in his, Mark used it to run up and down his length. Never before had Mark felt his ex-roommate's touch on his cock. It made his entire body shiver with forbidden delight.

"Stop."

Mark released his hold on Jack's wrist. Jack stayed connected to his dick for a moment longer before he gave it one last stroke and dropped his hand to his side.

Adam asked through the door, "Are you guys alive in there?"

"Yes," Jack answered quickly. "I have to go," he whispered to Mark.

"I know."

After staring at Mark's exposed cock as he backed up, Jack tore his eyes away and opened the door.

A minute later Steve pushed in.

Mark gasped and faced the wall. "Steve! Let me change."

"I just wanted to say I'm sorry." Steve touched Mark's back gently.

Mark discreetly slipped his cock into his bathing suit.

"I acted like a jerk. I thought we were roughhousing. Honest. I didn't think I was upsetting you."

"All right." Mark sighed, his back still facing Steve.

"Mark?"

His eyes to the ceiling looking for strength when he knew damn well he had no reserves to draw from, he turned to face his lover.

"I'm sorry, baby." Steve brushed his fingers against Mark's cheek. "Am I forgiven?"

"Yes. Of course."

Very slowly Steve sank to his knees and flipped Mark's soft penis out of his bathing suit. As it entered Steve's warm mouth, Mark imagined Jack in Steve's place, hating himself for tempting Jack to cheat on Adam.

Mark emerged from the bathroom, showered and changed into his clean gym shorts. He found the other three in the kitchen. Steve reached out for him. Mark leaned against Steve's legs as Steve sat on a high stool and watched Jack and Adam preparing dinner.

"You okay?" Adam asked Mark softly.

"I'm fine. Thank you, Adam." Mark's eyes darted to Jack's.

Jack gave him a brief glance, continuing to cut up vegetables for a salad. "Anyone need a beer?" he asked.

"Sure." Steve hugged Mark against his chest.

"Mark?" Jack's expression was so adoring, Mark felt his heart melt in admiration for him.

"Yes, love. Cheers."

Jack took three bottles out of the refrigerator along with iced mugs. He filled them and set them on the island counter they were all crowded around.

Adam marinated four thick steaks with a pastry brush and bowl of homemade barbeque sauce. "Is the grill ready, Jack?"

"Should be."

"I'll be back." Adam carried the platter of meat to the patio.

Steve reached around Mark for a beer mug. Mark leaned forward but Steve's knees held him from going too far away and one of Steve's arms was still wrapped around him tightly. Mark sometimes felt like a possession. Was that bad? He didn't know. It was better than being unloved. At least he was a valued possession.

But he couldn't help but wonder at Jack's thoughts as he witnessed it. Was Jack jealous? Did he cringe every time he saw it? Steve was like a Rottweiler when it came to territory. Mark felt as if he were a fire hydrant coated in his piss. *Do I make Steve insecure? Or is this just how he shows me he loves me? Should I ask Sonja what he did with her?*

"Ah!" Mark jumped when Steve touched the icy mug to the bare skin of his back.

"Sorry. An accident."

"It's okay." Mark used the opportunity to move away from Steve's hold. Able to stand on his own, Mark lifted his own beer mug to his lips. "Can I help you at all, Jackie?"

"I'm nearly done, Mark. Thanks." Jack cleaned the cutting board of carrot peels and limp lettuce leaves, running the garbage disposal.

Adam shouted through the screen door, "How do you like your steaks?"

"Rare," Steve answered.

"Medium." Mark looked at Jack and smiled. "Like you."

"Two medium, one rare," Jack relayed.

"Okay. Almost there, guys."

"Shall I set the table?" Mark asked sweetly, wanting to make sure he and Jack were okay after what had happened in the bathroom.

"Sure. Thanks." Jack dug through a drawer for the cutlery and silverware.

Mark had to move closer to Jack to retrieve the items. He brushed against Jack's arm. Jack met his eyes instantly. Mark gave him his most charming glance. As Jack handed off the knives and forks, Mark made sure their hands overlapped. "I got it, love," Mark whispered sensuously.

"Thanks."

Adam returned with a steaming platter of steaks. "Let's go."

Jack set plates around the table and Mark allocated the silverware to each place setting.

With a set of tongs, Adam doled out the cuts of meat. "One rare, two medium."

"Looks great, Adam." Steve set his beer mug down and licked his lips.

"Enjoy."

Jack placed the salad bowl with a basket of rolls in the center of the table.

"Thanks, Jackie." Mark winked at him while he cut his steak.

"My pleasure."

Mark ate, his eyes settled first on Jack, then on Steve. He wanted them both. Why was that too much to ask? Life wasn't fair.

A vision swept him up. Instead of Keith and Carl in a threesome it was him, Steve and Jack. Jack kneeling behind him, fucking him hard, Steve's cock in his mouth at the same time, fucking him orally. Mark imagined hearing both Jack and Steve climaxing, having them shoot their load into him simultaneously. Mark's cock grew stiff in his shorts.

Still in his dream world, after their orgasms, Mark would lie on the bed, Jack and Steve alternating sucking his cock and kissing him, both sets of hands touching him everywhere at once. Jack would whisper loving words into his ear while Steve gave him a blowjob, then they'd switch roles. Mark wanted to see what Jack looked like when he gave someone head. If Jack sucked him, Mark could feel his technique, learn if it was unusual, if Jack had any special talents.

"Mark?"

"Huh?" Mark blinked.

"The food all right?" Adam asked.

"The food?"

"Yes. You've stopped eating. Lost in thought?"

Mark looked around the table. They were all staring at him curiously. He sliced another bite from the steak and stuck it into his mouth to chew. Steve's hand found his thigh under the table. Soon it would find his hard-on.

While Steve's mischievous fingers spider-crawled their way to his crotch, Mark walked his toes towards Jack. When Mark bumped into Jack's bare foot, Jack jerked his head up.

Sensuously stroking Jack's foot with his, running it around Jack's ankle and calf, Mark had his cock squeezed by Steve at the same time. *Yes. Like this. Us three.*

Jack gave Adam a nervous glance. Adam appeared oblivious, consuming the food. Jack shot Mark an admonishing look, but didn't move away from Mark's contact.

My two men. Yes. Perfect. Maybe Adam can go out of town on business for a week or two.

Steve leaned to whisper into Mark's ear, "What got you so hard?"

"Hush," Mark chided, seeing the other two curious as to what was said.

"What are you two up to?" Adam laughed. "You're worse than rabbits in heat."

Steve's hand left Mark's lap and reappeared back on the table again, lifting his beer mug. "Sorry. Got sex on the brain."

"Is that like mad cow?" Adam chuckled, looking at Jack.

Mark had his toes riding up Jack's bare leg to his thigh. Any minute now Mark would look like he was balancing on one foot. As discreetly as possible, Jack reached under the table, gave Mark's ankle a squeeze and nudged it down to the floor again.

"You okay?" Adam asked Jack. "Why do I feel like I'm missing something here?"

Before Adam could peek under the table, Mark set his foot back in front of him.

"What are you missing, Adam?" Mark asked glibly.

"Why don't you tell me?" Adam seemed amused, not upset.

Mark assumed it was because he had no idea what was going on. "Me?" He batted his lashes coquettishly. "How would I know? I'm innocent."

Both Steve and Jack choked on their food.

As Adam gestured to the obvious rebuttal to Mark's dubious answer, Mark blushed.

"Mark…" Steve regained his composure after a laughing fit. "Putting your name in a sentence with the word innocent is an oxymoron."

"No kidding," Jack affirmed. "Give us a break, Mark Antonious."

"I love it when you call me that." Mark fluttered his long eyelashes again while leaning across the table towards Jack.

"Behave." Jack pointed his knife at him.

As if the notion were absurd, Steve quipped, "Yeah, right. Asking Mark to behave is like asking a baby not to shit his diaper."

"Oy!" Mark sat back. "That's crass. We're eating dinner."

"Are we?" Adam asked skeptically. "Or are we flirting shamelessly with two men?"

Mortified he'd been seen through, Mark had to keep reminding himself that Adam was in the business of knowing dirty little secrets. Hollywood agents were as keen as bloodhounds.

"Two?" Steve obviously wasn't as astute as the show biz hotshot. "Which two?"

"Forget about it, Steve." Jack resumed eating. "If you analyze it, you'll make an issue out of it. And I'm too tired for any more issues involving..." Jack stared at Mark intentionally and enunciated, "Mark Antonious."

"Oh! You're giving me an erection. Stop saying that." Mark licked his lips sensuously while staring at Jack.

Adam moaned, "Please don't tell me you want Jack again."

"What?" Steve seemed to be a page behind the action.

"I love all my men." Mark pushed his plate aside.

"How many men do you consider 'yours'?" Adam asked, sipping his drink.

Mark was afraid to answer. He'd already put his foot in it by his blatant flirting. Yet he couldn't resist. He liked being the center of attention. *So sue me.*

"One!" Steve answered for him.

"Oh?" Adam gave Mark a perceptive look.

Mark suddenly imagined Adam bringing up Carl Bronson and Keith O'Leary. "No. Adam, don't."

"Don't what, Mark?" Adam replied smugly, continuing to eat his meal.

"Yes." Jack leaned towards Mark across the table. "Don't

what, Mark?" he echoed with venom.

That shut Mark down instantly. His skin prickled with warning from Adam. Adam was very smart. Adam would find a way to control him. And he had.

Adam took his time, chewing leisurely, sipping his ice water. "Don't talk about those two actors? Is that what you don't want me to do?"

"It was a show. I did a scene with them." Mark shivered at Jack's unfriendly glare.

"Yes, Mark. Whatever you say, Mark." Adam's condescending air made Mark hate him suddenly.

"Are you done?" Mark asked Steve, pushing away his barely touched meal.

As Steve finished his food, he replied, "You want to leave now?"

"Yes. I'm tired." Mark averted his eyes from Adam's glance.

"Fine." Steve ate the last few bites of his steak. "Hate to eat and run, but..."

"You're eating and running?" Adam's smirk was driving Mark crazy. Mark wanted to strike him, wipe it off his face.

"Looks that way." Steve scooted out his chair and carried both his and Mark's plates to the sink.

Mark stood and stared at Jack sadly. *I can never have you. I had my chance and I didn't take it.*

Jack's expression dropped, almost as if he had heard those words Mark had tried to transmit telepathically.

Before he once again got sappy and teary-eyed, Mark moved away from the table. "Thank you both. It was a nice dinner."

"You're very welcome." It seemed all Adam's words were tinged with sarcasm suddenly. He had found Mark's Achilles' heel, toppled the giant with his slingshot, cut Sampson's long locks.

Mark walked behind Jack's chair as he went to meet Steve in the kitchen. He rested his hand on Jack's enormous deltoid muscle and said softly, "Thank you, Jackie."

"Let me walk you guys out."

Mark figured Adam was most likely still leering at him behind his back. He hooked Jack's arm at the elbow and was escorted to the front door. "Don't listen to Adam's nonsense."

"You let me worry about Adam."

Mark knew too many ways of interpreting that line and didn't have the chance to ask for it to be clarified.

Steve appeared with their canvas bag of wet swimsuits and towels. "Ready?"

"Yes." Mark leaned against Jack's broad chest and pecked his lips. "Goodbye, love."

"Bye, Mark."

"Goodbye, Mr. Lewis." Mark waved at Adam as he stood by, watching and taking everything in like a detective.

"Goodbye, Mark," Adam replied politely.

"See ya." Steve shook both their hands and waved as he stepped outside in the heat.

"You drive, copper." Mark tossed Steve his car keys. Mark peeked back at Jack where he stood at the door and noticed Adam wrapped around the big, beefy blond. *My beefy blond.*

The car was an oven. They both opened the doors and Steve gingerly reached in and started the engine, turning on the air. Steve spread out the two towels on the leather seats and got in, cringing.

Mark reached to feel the vents before he climbed in the car to make sure cool air was blowing out of them. He sat down, singeing his legs on exposed leather upholstery, quickly fixing the towel to cover the seat better. He closed the door and cranked the fan up to full blast.

Once Steve had them on the road, he asked, "What's going on between you and Jack?"

"Nothing. Ignore Adam. He's stirring things up."

"Why would he stir things up?"

"Leave it. I'm shattered and tired of debating my every flippin' move." Mark knew he only had himself to blame. He couldn't help it. He loved too hard and craved affection after a childhood without it. Even his psychiatrist couldn't fix him. Years he visited that man, paying him two hundred an hour to vent his woes. The moron did nothing but prescribe him Prozac. That was his big fix.

"You have to get over the events of your childhood."

"How can I? They affect every decision I make as an adult."

"You must take responsibility for your actions."

"I do. I am responsible. But my father sent a whore to my bed when I was thirteen. He kept trying to force women on me to prevent what he felt was the atrocity of having a homosexual son. When I resisted his attempts, he kicked my ass."

"You're a twenty-five-year-old man, now, Mark. No longer a child."

"My body has become twenty-five. But don't you get that my emotional state is still thirteen?"

"Are you depressed?"

"Yes!"

"Suicidal?"

"Chronically!"

"Then I will give you a prescription."

"Pills? That's your answer? Take pills? What about all these issues I have to deal with? I can't make a decision alone. Do you understand? If I didn't have Jack living with me, I'd fall apart."

"Does Jack resent you leaning on him for support?"

85

"I don't think so."

"Then lean on him."

"Lean on him."

"What?" Steve asked, cruising on the highway.

"Nothing." Mark rubbed his forehead in frustration. "Nothing at all."

Chapter Eight

Mark was beyond exhausted. The day felt long and tiring, both physically and mentally, and the heat was unbearable. Steve parked the TVR in the garage. Mark climbed out and scuffed his flip-flops to the connecting kitchen door. As the garage door lowered, blocking out the light, he entered their home and kicked his sandals off.

"I'm shattered. I'm having a lie down." Mark left the room.

"Okay." Steve's voice sounded apprehensive. Even in his one-word answer Mark could hear it.

While he climbed the stairs to the bedroom, Mark checked his watch. It was still early and broad daylight. He walked around the perimeter of the room, closing the heavy curtains, shutting out the sunshine. It was comfortable from the air conditioning pumping constantly but he turned on the ceiling fan as well to cool off his boiling hot skin. With a thud, he dropped down on the bedspread, crushing the pillow under his head and tried to rest.

He needed to leave Jack alone. Coming on to him was only going to mess them both up. *Forget it. You had your chance for almost two decades. It's not going to happen.*

"I'm a fool." Mark rubbed his face against the cool, crisp cotton pillowcase, brushing his wet eyes to dry them.

Steve was very supportive. Mark knew that. Whatever

G.A. Hauser

Mark needed, Steve would provide. But Jack always seemed the calmer of the two. More stable, reliable. Steve was a bursting force of male testosterone, exploding like a sexual firecracker.

Mark would not use the words "calm, stable influence" to describe ex-Officer Miller. More like "wild sex fiend". *But I love my Steven. Very much. I would never leave him, ever.*

He knew damn well the thoughts in his head were going to prevent him from settling down to a nap. He moaned, tossing to his back. Steve was watching him from the doorway.

Mark gazed at him dreamily. The man was gorgeous. He was the poster child for Uncle Sam's Army, the guy you envisioned when you thought of a Formula One Racing Champion, or the proud cop in a crisp, blue uniform. Clean cut, wholesome, sandy brown hair, brilliant blue eyes, perfect teeth, and high cheekbones. Steven Jay Miller was fanfuckingtastic. *Why am I looking anywhere else?*

"Hey."

"Hey," Mark responded.

Steve approached the bed, sitting down on it, touching Mark's leg softly. "Can't sleep?"

"No. But I do need to rest."

"Can I join you?"

"Of course."

The mattress shifted with Steve's weight. He drew Mark tightly against his body, curling an arm under Mark to seal him to his chest. Mark felt his stress dissipate at the comfort of the hug. Steve burrowed into his hair. Mark could hear him inhaling deeply, sniffing his scent.

A solid mound pressed into Mark's bottom. Chills covered his skin as Steve made him aware of how much he turned him on. His eyes closed, Mark felt the soft blasts of air on his face from the spinning fan. He was finally comfortable. Not overheated.

Steve began caressing his hair affectionately, combing

88

through its length, sending tingles over his skin. Mark released a deep, relaxing sigh.

It was what he needed to begin drifting off, feeling at peace for a fleeting moment. Mark had everything he needed and had to stop the eternal search for that Holy Grail.

Steve's loving touch ran down Mark's arm to his hip. Steve nuzzled the nape of his neck through his hair. Those tantalizing fingers slid inside Mark's gym shorts, under the elastic waist. When they paused at Mark's pubic hair, Steve petted the curls gently.

The sensation was so enticing, Mark emitted a quiet moan.

Steve shifted behind him, pushing his erect cock against Mark's ass crack. At the same time, Steve's palm cupped over Mark's soft package, kneading it lovingly.

Mark was aware he wasn't going to get his nap as planned. It seemed Steve couldn't resist a chance at lovemaking.

He didn't mind one bit. In fact, he loved it.

Soft kisses touched the back of his neck. A tongue swirled to his shoulder and Steve's mouth closed over his skin to suck on it.

After giving Mark's genitals a squeeze, Steve removed his hand. A second later he lowered Mark's shorts from behind, sliding his hard cock against the skin of Mark's bottom.

Mark couldn't help but smile. Steve's tactics for sex varied from a frenzied assault to this type of slow seduction.

Once Steve had positioned his dick to be able to slide between Mark's butt cheeks, Steve's fingers found their way again to the front of Mark's shorts. When he felt Mark's semi-erection, Steve wrapped around it and began stroking it as he pumped his hips.

Mark's heart beat faster and he opened his lips for a deeper breath. *That's it, baby. That's it.* He lived to please him. *Take me. Take me deep.*

Steve bent his top leg, resting it over Mark's hip for closer

89

G.A. Hauser

contact to his ass. "I need to fuck you."

It was said as an apology. More like, "Sorry, you can't nap yet." Mark was flattered he made Steve so hot that they couldn't even lie next to each other without fanning a spark.

"Yes. I want you in," Mark breathed, barely audible.

As if he needed to hear the approval first before getting too aggressive, Steve ground his dick into Mark's bottom for a few moments, pausing to reach into the nightstand.

His eyes closed, facing away from Steve, and completely relaxed, Mark listened, picturing Steve's movements. Steve removed his clothing, the foil package was opened, Mark's shorts were yanked down his legs. Mark was pressed face down on the bed and Steve's muscular arm wrapped around his hips, raising his buttocks.

At the penetration, Mark shivered in delight. Steve had his hand clamped around Mark's cock, but he wasn't satisfying it. More likely, satisfying himself with the feel of it.

His eyes still closed, Mark visualized Steve's expression as he climbed the ladder to climax. He knew it well. That luscious male grunting began, Steve turning into a savage beast. Mark's cock was squeezed deliciously as Steve thrust his hips deep and fast.

A ripple from Steve's cock pulsated throughout Mark's body. Another deep, jutting thrust inside and Mark knew it sent Steve spinning into a climax. Steve's hard shaft shuddered inside him. Steve prolonged it, moving in and out slowly but just as deeply. His hand began smoothing along Mark's length, just teasing it.

Steve caught his breath. His hips stilled but he did not back up. Mark assumed Steve was staring at the connection. *His cock in my ass.*

His low hiss reached Mark's ears. "I don't want to pull out."

Mark smiled contentedly. "Don't."

90

Before Steve disconnected their bodies, he ran his thumb over the tip of Mark's cock, smearing the pre-come drop around his head.

After a moment, Steve released him. Mark looked over his shoulder. Steve was working on removing the rubber. To get comfortable, Mark rolled to his back and watched Steve walk to the bathroom to wash up. Mark tugged his shorts back up his legs again. When Steve returned he crawled over the bed to him. "Want me to suck you off?"

"I'm good." Mark smiled at him.

"I'll let you nap." Steve kissed Mark's forehead and left the room.

Once the sound of Steve's footfalls receded, Mark felt lonely at his departure. He closed his eyes and could still feel Steve's presence inside him, like a luscious memory.

Finally allowed to rest, Mark fell into a deep slumber.

Chapter Nine

Monday morning, back at his office, Mark sat at his desk in front of his computer. His mobile phone rang. He dug it out of his suit jacket pocket and checked the LCD display. "Hullo?"

"Mark? Arnold Newhouse."

"Yes, hello, Arnold. How are you?"

"I'm great. I have the photos here from the session you had with Lorenzo."

"Oh?"

"They're spectacular. I emailed several out to some clients as teasers, and I already got a request for you to do a magazine ad."

"Really? That's quick. What does it advertise?"

"Cologne."

"Right." Mark looked at his open door. His coworker Charlie walked past with a cup of coffee in his hand.

"The appointment is for Wednesday evening. I told them you work full time and will only be available nights and weekends. It didn't seem to cause a problem."

Mark slid a piece of paper in front of him and raised a pen. "Okay, where and when?" As he wrote the information down, excitement stirred inside him. "Will they provide the clothing?"

"They may. I suggest wearing your snazziest business suit

anyway."

"Great. Thank you, Arnold."

"This is the first of many, Mark. I have a feeling you're going to become very hot property very soon."

His cheeks burning with the compliment, Mark laughed. "That's very flattering of you."

"You wait. You may not have to work the day job."

"Thanks again."

"My pleasure. Let me know how it goes."

"I will do." He hung up and spun back to his computer, his smile broad on his lips.

As noon approached, Mark leaned against the doorframe of Steve's office.

"Hey, good lookin'." Steve winked at him.

"You ready for lunch?"

"In a minute. What have you got in mind?" Steve continued to type on the computer keyboard.

"Something light. My appetite left with the cooler weather." Mark stood behind Steve's chair, massaging his shoulders through his dress shirt.

"Oh, yes. Your touch sends shivers right to my dick."

"Sh, we're at work." Mark peeked at the open door.

"Can't help it."

"I know. I suppose it doesn't make a difference. I imagine the staff must be used to us groping each other by now." Mark chuckled. "Anyway, Arnold Newhouse rang."

"And? Got your first prostitution job?"

"Will you give it a rest?" Mark shook him, continuing to rub his shoulders again. "It's for a cologne ad. That sounds very classy to me."

"When do you have to do it?"

"This Wednesday evening. At seven."

"Do you want me to come with you?"

"No. That would look very silly." Mark gave his shoulders a last squeeze and sat on the corner of Steve's desk.

Steve sent the email he was working on and swiveled in his chair to face Mark. "What if it's not classy? What if it's scary?"

"Shut up. Are all you ex-cops so paranoid?"

"You want to take my gun?"

"No. You sound like a hysterical mother. Stop it at once." Mark folded his arms.

Steve leaned his forearms over Mark's lap. "I worry about you."

"And I appreciate it, but I'm not a helpless female. Please stop treating me like one."

As someone passed by the open door, Steve sat up, moving off of Mark's thighs.

"Right. Lunch."

Steve followed him down the hall. "I want to know where this appointment is, and the phone number and name of the contact."

"You're being ridiculous." Mark exited the office to wait for the elevator.

"Indulge me."

Mark waited until they were alone on the elevator before he replied angrily, "Indulge you? I will not. You act as if I'm some weak twit who can't defend himself. It's rude and insulting. And I resent you for it."

"Ooh, you're getting all British on me again," Steve purred, snaking his arm around Mark's hips. "You know it turns me on."

"Everything I do seems to turn you on, Officer Miller." Mark raised his eyebrow at him.

As Steve humped Mark's body he moaned, "I'd fuck you

right here if I could. Suck me off in the car."

"No, Steven. Behave. We're nearly at the parking garage." But the thought made Mark smile wickedly.

"Please?" Steve rubbed his stiff cock against Mark's hip, licking Mark's neck.

A shiver raced over Mark's skin. "We had rules about touching at work. Remember?"

"Let's break the rules. We have in the past." The door opened and forced Steve to stop.

Mark headed to the car, feeling Steve's leer on his ass. "Oh, Steven, whatever shall I do with you?"

"Now who sounds like a mother?" Steve opened the car door.

Mark sat in the passenger's seat. Steve slid over and pulled him into a kiss. "What's got you all revved up?" Mark gasped as he was groped.

"You. Modeling." Steve chewed Mark's jaw.

"Why on earth would that excite you?" Mark couldn't control Steve's passion.

"It just does. I like the idea of other people ogling you but of only me fucking you."

Mark laughed softly.

"Suck me off. It'll take two seconds." Steve was already opening his suit trousers.

"I want to, love. You have no idea, but—" Mark took a paranoid glance around the area, "—if someone sees us, we'll never live this down."

Steve gripped the back of his neck and was urging him towards his lap and his protruding cock.

Mark resisted at first, then took one look at his lover's erection. "You are irresistible, love." He enveloped Steve's dick hungrily.

"Ah! Oh, holy Christ, Mark, you are the best fucking

G.A. Hauser

partner a man could ever have."

It was difficult to laugh with his mouth full. Mark sucked fast and strong in order to get this act over with before a work colleague caught him.

Steve's legs went rigid like his cock as he pressed back into the bench seat. Both Steve's hands in his hair coaxed him to penetrate deeper.

Mark's own cock throbbed at the risqué deed. Steve kicked his foot under the brake pedal and came, choking back his loud groans.

While Mark gulped down the load quickly, the quantity of sperm his lover ejaculated surprised him. He made sure he had swallowed it all then sat back, gaping at Steve in awe. He blinked. "Wow."

Steve leaned closer and licked the corner of Mark's mouth.

Mark quickly wiped his face, assuming some cream was present. "Christ, Steve."

"Too full for lunch now?" Steve laughed as he closed his pants.

"Yes, Jesus. You shot quite a load."

"I love you." Steve grinned wickedly at him, starting the car.

"You always say that when you've come inside me." Mark sat back and buckled his seatbelt, flipping down the visor to get at the mirror. He dabbed at his sticky chin in the reflection, cleaning off Steve's come. Once he was presentable, he sat back, folding the visor up. "I love you too, you madman." When Mark looked down he noticed a slight damp stain on his crotch. "Great."

"What?" Steve asked as he backed out.

"Nothing. You just get me so hot I stained me trousers."

"Heh, heh." Steve gave him a wicked glance. "You fucking love it."

"Make no mistake," Mark crooned sensually, holding Steve's hand. "I bloody well do." He kissed Steve's cheek.

The evening run had been brutal. Mark felt as if he was getting heatstroke. Four miles in the grueling sun. He once again stuck his head under the kitchen tap to cool off when they entered the house. "There has to be a better way than this."

Steve handed him a bottle of water as Mark leaned against the counter and his hair dripped, running down his naked torso. "We should join a gym where we can run in the air conditioning."

"That's for sissies." Steve guzzled his water.

"Or what if we turn the study into an exercise room? Like Jack has?" Mark panted to catch his breath.

"No. It'll suck. I like running outdoors. I always run outside."

"I get too overheated. It can't be good." Mark pushed his soaked hair back from his forehead.

"It's twenty minutes. Big deal." Steve tossed his empty plastic bottle in the trash. "See you in the shower."

After Steve left the room, Mark sipped the water, getting his breathing and heart rate back to normal. He picked up his mobile phone from the kitchen table and noticed the message symbol. He held it to his ear and heard Arnold Newhouse's voice. "Mark. Arnold here. I've got three more jobs for you. They're beating down my door, Mark. I told you. Call me and I'll give you the list."

Mark chuckled to himself and hit the delete button. Another voice came through the line at a second message.

"Mark? Keith. Uh, you want to get together with Carl and me again soon?"

"No!" Mark deleted it, shut down his phone, and tossed it on the table. "Bloody hell." He crushed the empty water bottle, hearing it crackle. "Like I'm not wracked with enough guilt over that incident."

He entered the bedroom and heard the shower running in the master bath. With Keith's voice reverberating in his head, he took off his running shorts and jockstrap. He entered the steamy bathroom and lifted the toilet lid to urinate.

Steve slid back the shower door to see him.

"Perv." Mark gave his dick a shake and closed the toilet lid.

"Get in here. What took you so fucking long?"

Mark climbed into the tub. "I checked my mobile messages." Steve began soaping up Mark's genitals vigorously. "You do realize that's not the only part of me that needs cleaning."

"I'll get to your ass in a minute."

Mark laughed in amusement. "You are insatiable."

"You love it."

"That's beside the point." Mark moaned at the handling his nuts were receiving. "Anyway, Arnold said I have three more appointments for modeling gigs."

"Really? Man, he didn't waste any time." Steve ran his hands, palm over fist, along Mark's cock.

A rush of fire racing over him, Mark reached for the walls to brace himself. "You treat me as if I were still twenty. I'm old. I can't keep up this pace you've set for me," Mark teased, tongue in cheek.

"Shut the fuck up." Steve's attention was on his task. "I'm keeping you primed."

"You're wearing me dick out."

"Does it feel good?"

"Yes."

"Then quit complaining." Steve held Mark's cock at the base, holding it upright. "What a prick you have. Have you ever measured it?"

"Measured it? Don't be absurd."

Steve trapped his own against Mark's, stroking them together. "Bet it's at least nine inches. Possibly ten."

"Why is everyone so obsessed with size?" Mark closed his eyes in delight as Steve nestled their cocks together, jacking them off as one. It didn't take long for a shiver to rush up his spine. Mark gripped over the top of Steve's hand and jerked with him.

The sounds of the water rushing into the tub and their gasping breaths were the only things Mark could hear at the moment. His balls tightened up while he climaxed. "I'm there, love."

At Mark's announcement, Steve's hand worked them harder. Steve came, clamping both his hands snugly around their shafts, a few strokes more and Steve's sperm ran down both their fingers as well.

Mark recovered and Steve licked the running water off Mark's chest, fingering his balls gently.

Mark was so sated sexually, he couldn't imagine going a day without a climax. At least that was the one thing in his life he wasn't frustrated over.

Chapter Ten

Wednesday evening Mark stood in front of the full-length mirror in his walk-in closet and knotted his silk tie. Steve sat on the bed in only his gym shorts, watching him. Mark moved to the highboy dresser and located his gold cufflinks, holding them out to Steve.

Steve fastened one into his stiff pale blue cuff. "What's the address?"

"Steve. Stop treating me like a child."

"Why can't you just give me the information? Why are you making an issue out of it?" Steve dragged Mark's other arm over his lap to fasten his second cufflink.

"Me making an issue out of it? Oh, that's rich." Mark checked that both links were in properly and took his suit jacket off its hanger.

"Leave your cell phone on."

"No. I'll be in the middle of a photo shoot. I can't have it ringing." Mark buttoned his suit jacket and tugged at it to lie properly.

Steve stood in front of him, fixed his tie and untucked his long hair from his collar. "I'll be worried sick."

"Over nonsense. Stop treating me like a flamin' woman." Mark didn't want this argument. He had to look good, not infuriated.

Steve cupped Mark's balls and breathed, "You are my flamin' woman."

"Thanks, Steve," Mark snarled sarcastically. "Always a nice jab at my fragile male ego."

"How could you have a fragile male ego with a dick this big?"

In anger, Mark jerked his hips away from him, complaining as he walked out of the room. "Always about my bloody penis. That's what I am to him, a walking phallic symbol."

"I heard that!"

"Good!" Mark descended the stairs with Steve right behind him.

"Is it in LA?"

"Yes." Mark counted to ten in his head before he exploded. He slipped his shoes on at the door to the garage and grabbed his keys.

"Where? Downtown?"

"Steven," Mark threatened.

"Fine!" Steve held up his hands. "But when someone slips you a fucking date rape drug and you're lying flat on your back, don't say I didn't warn you."

"I don't need this." Mark opened the door to the garage and headed to his car. Once he was seated in the driver's seat, pushing the remote to elevate the door, he started the car with a roar and glared at Steve in the doorway. The tires squealed on the cement as he backed out of the driveway, and he hit the remote control button to close the garage door, hiding Steve from his sight.

As Mark drove, his stomach flipped in anxiety. *What if he's right? What if I'm being set up for something nasty?*

"Why do you have to put those awful thoughts into my head?"

A half hour through busy LA traffic later, Mark found a place to park on the street. It was still daylight out, due to the long summer days, but slightly more tolerable in temperature.

Mark armed his car alarm with a chirp and hurried to the main entrance of a six-story building right off Santa Monica Boulevard. Inside the lobby of the sleek modern office space, he searched for the name of the company on the directory. He used the elevator to get to the fourth floor, trying not to allow Steve's dismal thoughts to color this meeting.

He paused as he stepped out of the elevator, smoothed back his hair and tried to compose himself. He took a deep inhale for courage and opened the door to the lobby, immediately hearing voices just beyond the hallway. "Hullo?"

A man appeared at the doorway. "Mr. Richfield?"

"Yes." Mark extended his hand.

"I'm the director, Abe Stern. Come right this way. We're ready for you. You look fantastic."

"Thank you." Mark instantly felt comfortable. Abe escorted him to a large photography studio, complete with a stage, backdrop, spotlights and high-tech equipment, where a man and a young woman were busy preparing. They both stopped what they were doing when Mark walked in.

"Very nice!" the woman gushed.

Mark's cheeks grew warm. "Hello."

"I'm Jessica. I'm Jose's assistant." She pointed to the second man.

Mark shook both their hands. "Mark. Mark Richfield. Nice to meet you."

"You look perfect." Jose admired Mark's clothes. "We had something prepared if you came in jeans." He gestured at a rack of suits.

"Arnold Newhouse suggested I wear a nice business suit."

"Yes. Excellent." Jose touched his elbow and directed him

to the backdrop.

Jessica reached up to brush Mark's hair and patted a powder puff on his shine.

"Thank you," he whispered.

"No problem." Her smile was full of invitation.

As they fussed with spotlights and colored backdrops, Mark relaxed his tightly wound muscles, thinking Steve's warnings were completely groundless. Arnold had a respectable firm. His clients were legit. Steve didn't know what he was talking about.

"Okay, Mark," Jose addressed him. "Stand tall, one hand on your hip, the other relaxed at your side. Look at the far wall."

Jessica rushed over to adjust Mark's suit jacket to lie flat, racing away again.

"Perfect. Beautiful," Jose crooned while walking around Mark with his camera and clicking the shutter smoothly.

Mark felt a rush of pleasure. It was easy money and satisfied some deep emotional need he had to be admired and respected. He could never please his father, but he could please these people.

An hour and hundreds of poses later, they wrapped up the shoot. Though he was very tired, Mark was happy with the work. He spoke with Abe as the other two were busy with unloading the film from the cameras and straightening up. "Thank you. I enjoyed that," Mark said.

"We're looking for someone to be our trademark man."

Mark smiled, focusing on Abe's brown eyes.

Abe continued, "For each season we'll have a new advertising spread for the same product."

With a nod at Abe to let him know he was listening, Mark glanced back and found Jessica staring at him as she folded a drop cloth.

"It would mean an exclusive contract with us, Mark."

"I see."

"So, of course I'll let you and your agent talk it over."

"Yes. Of course." Mark caught Jessica's eyes again. She couldn't be more than in her mid-twenties.

"It was a pleasure meeting you." Abe reached out his hand.

"Yes. Likewise." Mark turned to the two in the room. "Goodnight."

Jessica raced over to him, holding out her hand. "Goodbye, Mark."

He smiled, seeing a flicker of infatuation in her eyes. "Goodnight, Ms. Jessica."

She smoothed her thumb over Mark's empty ring finger. "Not married?"

"But I am taken. It's very flattering though."

"Better luck next time." She released his hand.

Mark waved and exited the room to the hall. He smiled to himself. "You see, Steven? Nothing to worry about."

The TVR parked beside Steve's Mercedes in the garage, Mark walked into the house through the kitchen. He found Steve reclining on the sofa in the den, watching television. Mark stood in the doorway of the dim room and loosened the knot in his tie.

"How'd it go?"

"I was drugged, gang raped, and left to die."

"Shut the fuck up."

Mark laughed softly, though he could tell his lover was not in good humor. With a pivot of his heels, Mark climbed the stairs to their bedroom to undress.

As he dropped his cufflinks into his jewelry box on the highboy dresser. Steve entered the room and sprawled out on the bed, his hand stuffed down the front of his gym shorts as Mark took off his suit.

"It went very well. So well, in fact, the director asked if I would be interested in an exclusive contract to be their cologne man."

Steve didn't reply. He was gripped to his own already erect dick. The head of it poked out of the waistband of his red shorts.

"What did you do to occupy yourself? Jack-off to gay porn?" Mark hung his suit jacket up.

"You're better than watching gay porn."

"Really? Lost the thrill of viewing Angel Loveday videos?"

"Never."

Mark chuckled but was surprised at Steve's serious expression. He folded his trousers and hung them up with his suit jacket.

"They make you change clothing?"

"No. They shot me in what I wore. Arnold had a feeling they would." Mark opened the buttons of his pale blue shirt.

"I'm surprised they didn't ask you to change anyway, just to get a look at you."

Once he removed his shirt and tossed it on a chair, Mark stood in his briefs, staring down at Steve. "Why do you think everyone has an ulterior motive when it concerns me? Do you think people are incapable of acting in a professional manner in my presence?"

"I bet someone came on. How many people were there?"

"Three." Mark watched Steve's hand increase its speed on his cock. "Two men, one woman."

"And? No one made a pass? Come on. Be honest."

"The woman noticed I wasn't wearing a wedding ring and did mention it."

"Bingo."

"She was barely mid-twenties."

"So? You think you can't attract a younger woman? You

really are an idiot, Richfield."

"Stop degrading me. I had my fill of that from my father." Mark left the room to wash up for bed.

In just his briefs, Mark scrubbed his face, used moisturizer on his skin, brushed his teeth, and then relieved himself. When he finished up and turned off the light in the bathroom, he found Steve naked, lying on his side, still massaging his cock.

"You call me an idiot and now I'm supposed to take it up the ass for you?"

"Yes."

Mark climbed into the bed and faced him. "Do you ever think the way you speak to me sometimes is insulting?"

"You're ultra sensitive." Steve brushed the back of his hand against Mark's cheek.

"Do you ever wonder why?"

"You keep telling me it's from your old man."

"Do you want to know what he did to me growing up?"

"Hell no. I had my own old man to deal with."

Mark dropped to his back in frustration. "Jack lets me vent about him."

"I thought you said your father was dead?" Steve sealed his body against Mark's side.

"Yes. Dead but never forgotten."

"Whose fault is that?"

"His," Mark shouted.

"You're lucky. My old man is still alive. And if he knew about you? He'd kill us both."

"I don't know how you've kept it from him for this long."

Steve started playing with Mark's genitals. "It's because of what he did to me and Sonja. I told you about that. He caught us together about to go into a coffee shop and pulled his gun on me, in uniform, on duty."

"Yes, that's right." Mark did recall that conversation. "He was forced to resign."

"Early retirement." Steve stroked Mark's cock slowly.

"So? That whipped him into shape?"

"It made him very careful around me. Even after Sonja and I split up, he and Mom never asked about my social life any longer. I'm not even nagged about being a bachelor at thirty-two."

"Lucky you."

"No. Lucky you, Mark. You don't want my father gunning you down. Did your dad ever point a loaded gun at you?"

"No. He just called me a fag, sent sluts to my bedroom since I was thirteen, and kicked my ass when he felt like it."

"See? And you think you're the one who had it bad?"

At the comment, Mark gave Steve a weary glare and though it felt good, he nudged Steve's hand away from his cock. "I can't get it up, love. I'm shattered. Do you want me to satisfy you?"

"I want to satisfy you as well."

"I'm too tired. Honest, love. It's okay."

"I want your ass."

Mark grinned. "You always want my ass."

"Can I have it?"

Mark looked down as Steve jerked his rigid cock. "Of course, my pet." He rolled over and bent his knee so he was accessible.

Behind him Mark could hear Steve eagerly getting ready. A minute later, Mark felt Steve knocking at his back door. Mark closed his eyes. The familiar sensation of Steve's body merging with his always comforted his tired soul. While fondling Mark's entire body in a myriad of ways, Steve humped to his heart's content.

At one point Mark's dick grew erect and Steve jerked on it

while he thrust his hips, but Mark knew he was way too worn out to come. The wonderful sound of Steve's manly grunting and feeling Steve's cock once again trembling in his bottom made him smile contentedly. He sighed in exhaustion once Steve left to wash up.

When he returned, Steve spooned Mark from behind, cupping his hand over Mark's soft cock, and fell quickly to sleep. With the soothing sound of Steve's breathing behind him, Mark sank into a deep slumber.

Chapter Eleven

Thursday, after a quick dinner with Steve, Mark was again in his TVR Tuscan S, his pride and joy, and cruising this time to West Hollywood. Allowed to pass the gate at a studio lot, Mark remembered his stint on *Forever Young*. He never stopped feeling a sense of thrill at all things celebrity.

He was forced to park in a distant spot in the overcrowded lot. He checked his paperwork and felt hot in the business suit he was wearing. Arnold suggested he always show up dressed to the nines in case it was what the client expected.

Once he gave his name to a guard, Mark was allowed entrance and moved through a dim corridor on a concrete floor to a double door with a numbered sign over it. Studio twelve. When he opened it, he found a group of people, men in business suits, chatting together. Someone noticed him and tapped another man.

"Hullo?" Mark smiled shyly. "I'm Mark Richfield. Am I in the correct place?"

"Mark!"

At seeing a familiar face, Mark grew excited. "I don't believe it!" He rushed to Janis Campbell's outstretched arms for a hug and practically lifted her off her feet. "Janis!"

"Mark, you gorgeous hunk. You never change." Janis grabbed his hair and tugged on it. "When I read your name on the paperwork I almost died."

A wash of memories cascaded over him instantly. "You look superb. Honest, Janis, you still are the spitfire."

"Are you and Jack still together?" She gripped his hand.

The smile faded from his face. "No, love."

"What? Oh come on, Mark."

"It's a horrid, long, drawn-out tale that I am loath to tell."

"Okay. Never mind." She investigated all his fingers. "Not married."

"No."

"So, you are gay?"

"Yes." He chuckled from the nerves.

"I have to hear why you and Jack never stayed together. Are you still in touch?"

"Yes. We're close friends." Mark felt his heart break. Though he and Jack were only roommates, it was evident Janis had known something he hadn't at that time in his life.

She dragged him to the other members of the group. As she made hurried introductions in her frenetic way, Mark barely heard their names. He did notice an exceptionally handsome black fellow who was smiling sweetly at him. His name Mark caught. Theo.

"Right." Janis clapped her hands to either think or get everyone's attention. "Mark, since you just arrived, this shoot is for Ralph Lauren jeans, as you know, or don't know." She gave his clothing a once-over. "So, you and Theo need to change. Why don't you do that first and we'll discuss the ad when you're through."

Theo led the way to a young man near a rack of blue jeans on hangers. "Twenty-nine?" He held up Mark's size.

"Yes." Mark realized all his stats were included in his portfolio.

"Theo…thirty?"

"Thanks, man." Theo took the hanger, and he and Mark entered a small room wall to wall with mirrors.

As Mark removed his suit and shirt to hang on empty hangers, Theo asked, "Have you modeled long?"

"No, actually. This is my second gig."

"Really?"

Mark looked at Theo's reflection in the mirror. As Theo removed his shirt, Mark could see his powerful physique. "Yes. Really."

While Theo dropped his slacks, Mark averted his gaze politely.

When he was down to his briefs, Mark squeezed into the skintight jeans. "Are they supposed to appear painted on?"

"Apparently." Theo zipped his up and checked his rear view in a mirror.

Once Mark had his fastened, he asked, "Shoes?"

"I'll find out." Theo left the room for a moment.

Mark looked at his naked upper body and compared it to Theo's muscular chest, wondering if he appeared too slender in contrast.

"Bare feet." Theo poked his head into the room.

"Right." Mark tugged off his socks.

He and Theo rejoined the group. Janis lit up with excitement at their approach. "Perfect!"

Mark grinned contentedly, remembering her posing several naked men for her coffee table book. He wondered if she still dabbled in that field. He made a mental note to check Amazon when he got home.

With Janis's instruction, he and Theo sat like bookends, back to back, their knees bent and their arms intertwined as they pressed their palms onto the floor. At the touch of Theo's warmth, Mark felt a tingle of passion. Twisting to face forward where the camera was set up, Mark heard Theo giggle and

G.A. Hauser

whisper, "Your hair is tickling me."

"Oh, sorry, mate."

"I don't mind."

That seductive reply sent Mark's cock throbbing. Unfortunately, in the skintight jeans it had no room to move.

Janis knelt in front of them, fussing with Mark's hair so it fell in a soft uniform wave down both his and Theo's shoulders.

"Don't you two look scrumptious," she said.

Mark felt Theo's laugh like a rumble through his body. It surprised Mark that this macho black man was gay.

"Okay. Don't move." Janis raced to her tripod. "Don't smile. Look sullen, pout, you know."

Mark thought of Janis's comments regarding Jack and the pout formed instantly.

"You two are fantastic," she cheered like a coach at a soccer match.

Mark recalled every moment with her when he was twenty-one—the loitering with naked men, finally feeling normal around them as so many showed off the beauty of their perfect forms and shot their sensual glares at each other.

Janis stood them up and had them do the same thing standing, their backs pressed against each other, their elbows laced. Mark resisted an urge to squirm against Theo's fabulous body. His cock never softened during the entire shoot.

Around the perimeter of the makeshift stage, spotlights and backdrop, men stood staring. Mark assumed they were some representatives of the company making sure Janis did her job. The irony was that Janis could do that job better than anyone, and Mark hoped they were aware of her talent.

As Janis took a moment to reload her film, Mark stared at Theo and Theo back at him. They smiled warmly at each other. When Theo reached out to brush Mark's hair back from his eyes, his stomach flutter.

112

"You have a partner?"

"Yes." Mark breathed the word softly.

"Exclusive?"

"Yes." Mark tried to imagine what kissing Theo would feel like, but kept a rein on his horny dick. His life was complicated enough.

"You're fucking beautiful."

"You took the words out of my mouth."

"I'd love to suck the words out of your mouth."

"Don't get naughty. It's already killing me."

Theo made a deliberate appraisal of Mark's crotch. "I know the feeling."

Mark did the same to him.

"Damn jeans are so tight I'm dying."

With a smile, Mark replied, "I'm surprised my zipper hasn't exploded."

"I keep hoping it will."

Janis finished her task and stood straight. "Right." She closed in on them again. "Look at the two of you with your bulging crotches. It's so cute."

Mark glanced at the men on the exterior of their circle and covered himself with his hand.

"Stop. They're oblivious to gay men. They see dollar signs when they see you two, not anal sex."

Mark choked at her no-nonsense manner, momentarily forgetting the independent Janis Campbell.

"Please don't talk about anal sex," Theo whined.

"Sorry. Okay. Stand side by side, thumbs in waistband, weight on one leg."

Mark and Theo instinctively leaned towards each other. Janis nudged them so they met at the shoulder.

"Touching you is making me insane," Theo whispered out

of the corner of his mouth.

"Stop. You're killing me."

"Soften up your faces," she shouted. "You both look tortured."

"Bloody hell," Mark muttered, trying to change his sexual yearning to a more placid expression.

Forty minutes later, they were released from their session. Mark felt exhaustion moving in on him from full-time work and part-time modeling. While he shimmied out of the skintight denim jeans, he caught Theo eyeing him. *Oh, love, in another lifetime. Not this one. I'm already in a muddle.*

Once again in his suit, folding his tie and putting it into his jacket pocket, Mark exited the changing room and met Janis.

"What are you doing now?" she asked.

"I was going to go home."

"No. I have something you need to see. It's at my studio."

"Okay."

Mark heard Theo's voice. "Nice working with you, Mark."

Mark took his extended hand. "You too, love. A pleasure."

"Bye, Janis."

"Bye, Theo. Thank you so much. You were awesome." After she watched him go, she gripped Mark's hand. "Let me get my shit together, then I want you to follow me."

"All right."

In a few minutes Mark was seated in his car, driving behind Janis's Lexus to her place. Checking the dash, seeing the clock read nine fifteen, he had an impulse to ring Steve, but decided it wouldn't take him too long at Janis's and he'd just let it go for now.

She pulled into a driveway in Sherman Oaks in front of a large colonial-style mansion surrounded by high brick walls. Mark assumed it was not only her studio but her home. In the glow of security spotlights, he parked behind her car in the long, curved drive.

Before he exited his car, Mark took off his suit jacket to leave behind and rolled up the sleeves of his crisp dress shirt. Just realizing Janis was struggling with her gear, Mark hurried to help her carry her camera and equipment bags to the front door. She turned the lock and pushed back the door. Two German Shepherds greeted them, wagging their tails and snuffling at them in excitement.

"Hello, boys." Mark got a snout in the crotch and twisted away. "Where do you want these things?"

"Follow me." She led him to a back room, turning on lights as she went. "Set them there. Thanks."

Mark rested the cases on the floor and looked around. The walls were papered with snapshots, blown-up pictures and posters of Janis's book advertisements. He petted one of the dogs as it stood next to him, rubbing its ears playfully.

"That's George and Maggie." She pointed them out.

"Okay." Mark chuckled at their names. "They're lovely."

"You'll get covered in hair if you keep that up. Come here."

Curious what this was all about, Mark approached her. She opened a file cabinet and thumbed anxiously through the contents. Mark assumed he would be shown his own shots from the book he'd done with her, many moons ago.

"Here." She opened an envelope and handed him an eight-by-ten photograph. When he looked at it he almost fell over.

"Ah, you forgot about that one."

A sensation of dizziness washed over him. He checked the room for a chair and sat himself down to examine the photo more closely. "I did. I completely forgot about it. My God."

"That's why I thought you and Jack would still be together. Look at the two of you."

Instantly transported back to 1993, Mark remembered

115

taking Jack with him when he was first asked to pose for *American Male-Men*. Mark had been very nervous, especially when it came to taking off all his clothing for a camera. Jack willingly agreed to come. Always the steadfast friend.

While he and Jack sat in Janis's office as she discussed the contract and photo details, she commented on how handsome a couple they made. Playfully, Mark licked Jack's cheek to show him his affection. Janis had captured it on film. Sixteen years later, Mark was looking at it. And the expression on Jack's face floored him. Jack was glowing. His brilliant turquoise eyes were on fire. His blond hair was longer then, in wild, thick waves framing his handsome face. His eyebrows and sideburns were dark brown, making his expressions more intense.

"He was so in love with you."

That rattled Mark to his core. He set the photo on his lap, covered his face and was overwhelmed with sadness.

"Oh, Mark…" She rubbed his back warmly. "I didn't mean to upset you."

"What I did to him," Mark choked up in agony. "It was a crime."

"What? What did you do to him?"

"I loved him so much. I just was afraid to admit I was gay back then. I tortured him."

"Shh. Come on." Janis took the photo off his lap.

When Mark felt it move, he reached for it. "No. Please."

She handed it back to him. "Keep it."

As he stared at it, hot tears ran from his eyes.

"Who are you with now?"

"An ex-LAPD cop. Steve."

"I see."

"I adore him. I do. But Jack and I have so much history, Janis. You know that."

"I do. Can I get you a drink?"

"Yes. Please." When she left the room, Mark stared at the photo. He remembered Jack's taste. He didn't know what impulse at that time made him lick Jack like that, other than how much he adored him. "Jackie, I'm so sorry. What did I do? Oh, God."

Janis returned with a shot of cognac.

"Thank you, love." Mark's hands trembled as he held the glass.

"I never would have brought you here if I'd have known it would upset you, Mark. Forgive me."

Mark inhaled deeply, taking a moment to prepare himself. He shot down the alcohol. "I broke his heart. So much has gone on since this photo was taken. I've made such a cock-up of my life."

"How so?" Janis took the glass from him and set it on a nearby table. "You still look like a movie star, you're working as a model…"

"No. No, love. Socially."

"You don't have to delve into painful areas, Mark."

"If I do, I'll wail like a baby." Mark wiped at his eyes.

"Do you love Steve?"

"Yes. I do. I worship him."

"Then?" She pushed the hair back from his forehead.

"But he's not Jack. Jack and I had something very special. If I could, I'd go back and begin the physical relationship with Jack that he craved so much and was denied."

"Is Jack single?"

"No. He's found someone. He's settled."

"I suggest you let sleeping dogs lie."

When she glanced back at the two large canines doing just that, Mark smiled sadly. "Aye, yes. Don't wake the beast."

She returned to the file cabinet. Mark dabbed at his eyes while she hunted for more photos. A stack of proofs in her hand, she pulled a chair next to him. She handed him a magnifying lens to see the small shots clearly. "These are from our session together. Take a look. See if you'd like any of them for yourself."

Mark set the stack on his lap. "You know Jack has two copies of that book. Have you done more similar?"

"Yes. I've had one published every two years. I was fortunate enough to be invited to a set where a dozen young men were getting ready to be filmed in Israel. Gorgeous young men from all over the world were gathered there. It was exhilarating."

"I'll have to buy one of your books. I've not really had time to read lately."

"No reading, Mark. They're all just photos of nude men."

"Oh, darn!" Mark smiled. He took a moment and scanned the proof. "I look so young."

"You were. Twenty-one. A mere sprout."

"Why do we have to change?"

"You mean grow old?"

Mark nodded.

"That's life. Look, be thankful you won the genetic lottery and are still enjoying being one of the best-looking men on the planet."

He lowered the eyepiece. "How shallow is that?"

She shrugged. "It is if you're conceited. You have never been conceited."

"Vain. Very vain."

"So? Big deal."

With a deep exhale, Mark gazed at the stunning photographs of pretty boys surrounding him. "I'm so worried I'll shrivel up into a prune. I've begun to imagine Botox and surgery."

"Not yet." She touched his cheek. "You don't need a thing

at the moment."

"No. But forty is rearing its ugly head."

"Do what you have to do to keep peace in your mind."

Mark twisted on the chair to face her. "You never married, Janis?"

"I did. I'm divorced."

"What happened?"

"He was jealous. He thought just because I photographed beautiful men I slept with them and compared every perfect ten to him."

"Yes. I could understand that."

"I couldn't. I didn't think he was insecure when I married him."

"Aren't we all, deep inside?"

"No. Not all of us." She cupped Mark's face tenderly. "You always were. You punished yourself with everything you did."

"I still do."

"Let it go. You're only human. Humans have defects and frailties."

"That's all well and good until you hurt a loved one."

"I would agree only if you set out intentionally to harm."

Mark's teeth clenched for a moment from guilt. "I never set out intentionally. But I still know what I am doing is wrong when I do it."

"Ah, temptation. It lurks around every bend. Especially for the beautiful ones."

"I should wish I was born plain. But that's a lie. I know damn well I use sex to get what I want. But what else is there to me?"

"Don't go down that self-reproach route. You can't win that war."

He gazed at her affectionately. She had aged. She was more than ten years his senior, but she still had the sparkle of youthful vitality in her eyes. Yes, her hair was speckled with gray now, there were laugh lines near her eyes, but she was still beautiful to him. "I've missed you."

"I love how your eyes tear up when you say that, Mark. You are so loving and dear."

"You'll make me cry." Mark sniffed and dabbed his eyes in embarrassment.

"Take these home." She patted the stack of proofs on his lap. "Let me know if you want any of them made."

Mark looked down at the reminder of his youth and shook his head. He handed the pile back to her. "No. No, love. Just this one." He held up the one of he and Jack.

"Are you sure?"

"Yes. I told Steve I felt like Dorian Gray and these photos of my youth only remind me of what I am losing."

She rose up, setting the handful of sheets down on her desk. "I've enjoyed catching up with you."

"Aye. Me too, love. I'm so glad I've found you again."

She took the one photo from Mark and slid it into a manila envelope. With it she placed one of her business cards. "Don't be a stranger. I'm here anytime you need an ear."

"I do adore you." Mark hugged her tight.

When they approached the hallway the two dogs stood, wagging as they followed.

She kissed Mark's cheek at the door and waved.

The envelope in his hand, Mark sat in his car and waved back as he drove past her door in the arched driveway.

Before he made it home, Mark stopped his car. He wasn't ready to end the night yet. He had too much on his mind. He pulled the photo out of the envelope again. "Oh, Jackie-blue," he moaned sadly. "Why was I such a fool?"

Mark hid the picture before he sobbed like a baby. He found his tie and knotted it around his collar quickly, stepped out of his car, sliding his jacket on as he walked. He strolled to a club several blocks down the street. Pedestrians in colorful summer regalia were passing, laughing or talking in excited tones at the beauty of a summer night in LA.

When Mark stepped up to the door of a restaurant it was opened for him by an attendant. "Do you have a reservation, sir?"

"I just wanted a drink at the bar."

The man gave him a good once over before he decided. This restaurant was slightly over the top with its dress code and reservation rules. "Yes, come in. Enjoy."

"Thank you." Mark moved through the crowd to a dimly lit bar. He relaxed at a table for two and was immediately addressed by a waiter. "What can I get you, sir?"

"A shot of Cuervo, please."

The waiter bowed and left. Mark looked over the crowd. Several people were staring at him. This was the type of establishment that catered to the elite of Hollywood. Mark wondered if they thought he was someone. *I'm no one. Look the other way.*

He removed his mobile phone out from his pocket and held it to his ear. He listened to a message from Steve. "You still on the shoot? How long do those things go for?"

"No. I'm drugged, gang raped, and left for dead." Mark shook his head in annoyance. *My luck I will be one day. I better shut up.*

He had an urge to call to comfort his lover. When his drink showed up, he changed his mind. He removed the lime from the rim, sipped the tequila, then shot it back. At the sting of the strong booze he stifled a choke and chewed on the lime wedge. When he was done gnawing on it, he tossed it into the glass.

His eyes gazing off in the distance, he moved the empty

G.A. Hauser

glass across the table like a chess piece.

He looked at his phone again. Jack's mobile would be turned off. He'd be home. With Adam. Screwing Adam?

If Mark called his house, Adam would answer. He just knew Adam would. If he did, what would Mark say? He couldn't ask Jack out for a drink, could he?

Why not? Why couldn't he ask Jack out for a drink? It was only nine thirty. Surely Jack could come out for one.

A fresh shot was set before him. Mark spun around to look at the waiter's wry smile. "I didn't order another one, did I? Am I going mad?"

"No, sir. This is from the girls at that table."

Mark looked to where he pointed. Four twenty-somethings were giggling and waving at him. "Bloody hell. Can you tell them no thank you? I don't need the aggro, love."

"Sure." He picked it back up.

"But, uh, I would like one more."

The waiter set it back on the table. "I'll tell them."

"You're a sweetheart. Thank you."

The waiter gave him a flirtatious wink. Mark watched the man walk to the girls' table, pointing and seemingly explaining. There appeared to be some debate.

Mark cringed. He threw the second drink down his throat. "I have to get me a flamin' wedding band." He hid his hands under the table. *Jack. Can I call Jack and ask him to come out for one drink without everyone murdering me?*

"Bullocks." He dialed Jack's home number.

"Hello?"

"Jack, love."

"Hi, Mark. You okay?"

"I'm just glad it was you that picked up. Listen, Jackie, would it be terrible if you came out for one drink with me?"

"When?"

"Now? Tonight?"

"Where are you?"

"The Green Door."

"Is Steve with you?"

"No. No, love, I'm on me lonesome."

"I assume you want me alone, without Adam."

"Yes. You assume correctly. Will I get you into a mess? Don't do it if you'll get grief, Jackie."

"Yes. He'll be wondering why I need to do this."

"I need you. Please. Just for a chat." Mark looked back at the girls. They were staring at him rudely. He tilted his shoulder away from them.

"For a chat? And it has to be now?"

"No. Forget it, love. I know I'm a burden on your good nature."

"Hang on."

It sounded to Mark as though Jack cupped his hand over the phone. With all the background noise and music, Mark couldn't hear anything Jack was saying, presumably to Adam.

After a protracted length of time, Mark got the feeling Jack and Adam were arguing over it. "Jack. Jack…forget it. Jackie…" He rubbed his face in agony.

Another shot of booze appeared.

He raised his head. "I thought I mentioned I didn't want any drinks from them."

The young man stifled his laugh. "It's from a woman at the bar."

Mark spun around. An older woman with a slit in her skirt up to her hip was ogling him.

"Good heavens no." Mark handed him back the drink. "Send her my sincerest apologies, would you?"

G.A. Hauser

The young man took back the glass.

"Jack? Are you there?"

"I'm here." Jack sounded awful.

"No? Am I to assume you can't come?"

"I'll be there. Give me a few minutes."

"Strict dress code here, love. Jacket and tie."

"I remember."

Mark hung up, dropped the phone back in his pocket and wondered at the sacrifice Jack had just made to get out to see him at this hour. Adam must be livid. What on earth was he doing to Jack and why did he keep doing it?

"No! You have to be kidding me." Mark gaped at the fresh shot of tequila.

The young man couldn't hold his laughter any longer. Through his hysteria he pointed. "Old guy over there."

When he spun around, Mark found an elderly, well-dressed gentleman with a lascivious leer aimed his way.

"No. Please. No more attempts at me. If they ask, say no right off." Mark removed his wallet and shoved two twenties into the young man's hand.

"I'll try. Man, this is so damn funny."

"To you, love, only to you." Mark tried to face a wall to avoid any eye contact, running his hands through his hair nervously. *Why am I meeting Jack here? Why?*

He knew why. Perhaps Jack did as well.

What felt like an eternity later, Mark glanced up at the entry. A strikingly handsome blond wearing a tailored business suit was asking the host something. Mark rose up to get Jack's attention.

Just the sight of Jack made him salivate. It was Jack's beauty, intelligence and size that ignited his passion. Mark knew this was a bad idea. A very bad idea.

"Mark." Jack nodded, sitting down at the table with him.

124

"What have you been drinking?"

"Tequila shots."

"Are you toast?"

"No. Just had two. Buzzed, but not inebriated."

The waiter approached Jack. "What can I get you, sir?"

"Beer. Anything on tap."

"Would you like anything else?" he asked Mark.

"Ice water. Thank you."

"At least now the offers will stop." The young man smiled.

"Offers?" Jack asked.

"Never mind." Mark waved the waiter away.

"What's on your mind?" Jack leaned over the table towards him.

"I had another photo shoot this evening."

"And?"

"You'll never guess who I ran into."

Jack kept quiet, his eyes intense.

"Janis Campbell."

"Really? She still in photography?"

"Yes. Going strong."

"That must have been a nice reunion."

The waiter appeared with their drinks. When he left, Jack sipped his beer. "What was the shoot for?"

"Jeans. That's not what I wanted to talk about."

"I know what you want to talk about."

"Did Adam have a fit? Am I getting you into trouble?"

"Let me handle Adam."

Mark had heard that line before and he was still curious of the exact extent of what "handling Adam" would entail. "She had a photo, Jack."

"I assume she has millions of photos." Jack took another deep drink of his beer.

"Of us."

"Us?"

"Yes."

Jack reclined in his chair as if he was trying to recall it.

Mark leaned over the small table, waving Jack closer. "Remember when she was first explaining the project to me?"

As if it suddenly dawned on him, Jack nodded, a sweet smile on his lips. "I remember."

"She gave me that photo."

"Where is it?"

"In my car." Mark wanted him. His best friend, his soul mate, his confidant, his rock, he had to have Jack.

"I see." And according to Jack's expression, Mark knew damn well he did see. "What can I say?" Jack set the glass aside. "You made all the decisions."

"I did. But look at me. Have you ever known me to make a good one?"

"You regret meeting Steve?"

"No. Not at all. This has nothing to do with Steve."

"Nothing?" Jack's smile was ironic. "How wrong can you be?"

"God, Jackie..." Mark reached across the table to Jack's hands, clenching them in his.

A dark cloud passed over Jack's handsome face. "Why do you wait until we're both in a committed relationship to do this? Do you realize we had sixteen years together? Lived together? Did fucking everything together?"

"Not everything."

Jack dragged his hands back, releasing the hold. "That's not my fault."

"No. I take the blame. But think about it. I was petrified. My father made me scared of my own shadow."

"I know." Jack sipped his beer.

"That whole debacle with Sharon, that nightmare of pretending to be straight—"

"I know all about that too. And about you discovering anal sex on a business retreat with an ex-LAPD cop. Or do you want to remind me about that as well?"

Mark balled up his fists in frustration. "Yes. I know. I know."

With a last gulp, Jack finished his beer and wiped his lip with his napkin. "Can I see if I'm getting this straight?"

Mark's head began pounding. He picked up his ice water glass and ran it over his forehead to cool it.

"Now that I'm in a committed relationship with an awesome man, you want me. Am I close?"

"Stop. Jack."

Jack reached for the glass and moved it back to the table, using his napkin to dab at the water on Mark's forehead. "Not to mention, Steve is completely wild about you. Do you have any idea how much that man loves you?"

"Yes. Yes, I do."

"Do you love him?"

"Yes. Very much."

"What am I missing here?" Jack opened his hands in question.

The need to touch Jack was overwhelming so Mark reached his legs under the table to trap Jack's, then ground his jaw as he spoke the painful truth. "You. I am missing you. Never in those years did I taste your tongue in my mouth. Nor have I stroked your body in foreplay. I've never devoured your cock and tasted your come. I've never felt your mouth on mine. I yearn for the feel of your dick up my ass, of you jamming your body against mine so hard I feel a part of you. I need to hear the whimpering groans of you in orgasm…" Mark's eyes began to fill with tears. "I lived with you for sixteen years and all I did was tease you. I hate myself for what I had and what I lost."

Jack squirmed on his chair, his face showing some shock at what he was hearing. "You have to stop talking like that."

"To cuddle you after we've made love…for our sweat to mingle and overlap our hips, our chests." Tears began to run from Mark's eyes. "To sleep in your arms all night. To feel your morning erection poking me whilst I rest…"

"Mark…please."

"I had all of you and I had none of you." Mark bit his lip on a loud sob.

"We have to get out of here."

Mark stopped Jack from taking out his wallet. He set more than enough cash on the table and stood. With Jack at his side, they left the restaurant.

"Where did you park?"

"Far away. Several blocks."

"I'll walk you to your car." Jack held Mark around his waist. Mark immediately reciprocated, clinging tightly.

When they stood on the sidewalk by the TVR, Mark whispered, "Sit for a minute. Let me show you the picture."

A worn expression appeared on Jack's face. "Fine."

Mark unlocked the door and dropped into the driver's seat as Jack reclined in the passenger's. Mark set the envelope on his lap.

Once Jack shut the door, he stared down at it. "Do I want to see this?"

"You do."

After a deep breath, Jack slowly slid the photo out of its concealment. Mark stared down at it in the streetlight's glow. A moment later, Jack covered his face with both hands, weeping.

"Oh, God," Mark moaned, gripping Jack to him, crying with him. "I'm sorry. I made a mistake that will haunt me forever. Jackie. I had you! I had you! And I let you go."

Jack shoved the photo off his lap to the floor and collapsed over his lap in a *C* shape. Mark reached over the console and stick shift to embrace him. "Baby...oh, baby..." He kissed Jack's hair, his jaw. "Forgive me. *Oh, God*, forgive me..."

In an abrupt movement, Jack gripped Mark's face in an iron hold. Mark gasped at the shock of what was coming next. He expected to be shoved back, rejected. When Jack's mouth connected to his, Mark melted to the leather bucket seat.

The two of them were hysterical—crying, kissing between sobs and deep intakes of air.

"Mark...Mark..." Jack wept, kissing Mark's face and lips.

Mark grasped Jack's wrists, holding him still, finally able to enter Jack's mouth with his tongue. The instant Jack felt it, he seemed to go wild. Jack twisted in the confined space, dragging Mark even closer still, until Mark was impaled by the gearshift. The urge to be on Jack too urgent to deny, Mark climbed his way across the compartment and managed to get on his knees on the passenger's side and pressed against Jack between his straddled thighs. And they kissed. Kissed like he and Jack had wanted to kiss for the last nineteen years.

Jack's mouth tasted sweet, fresh, like the crisp ale he had consumed, combined with his own wholesome essence. His cologne and body scent brought back so many memories, Mark felt like a child again.

Jack's tongue boldly explored Mark's mouth, his teeth, his lips, his face, tasting everywhere he could reach.

"I love you. I love you." Mark couldn't stop the tears.

"God, I'm kissing you. I'm kissing you..."

Desperate for a breath, Mark dug his hands into Jack's thick blond waves and leaned their foreheads together. Jack was panting with the same intensity as he was.

"What the hell are we going to do?" Mark asked desperately.

"I don't know." Jack kissed him again, smoothing his hands down Mark's back to his ass, squeezing and massaging it.

"I don't want to hurt either Steve or Adam."

"I know, babe." Jack licked Mark's chin, kissing him again deeply.

In the awkward space and position, Mark tried to connect their crotches together. He straddled Jack's body and pressed into Jack's pelvis. That fabulous cock was like a stick of dynamite.

Mark rested his head on Jack's shoulder as Jack's hand explored him. When Mark felt it on his cock, rubbing through his trousers, it was like a fire had been set in his body. "My Jackie...I'm so sorry I messed us up. I'm such an idiot. Why didn't I respond to you? Why?"

"I think it's all about timing. You were petrified."

"I was, Jackie, I was." Mark sniffled as his tears renewed.

"And when you and Steve were alone in the desert, there was no one to judge you, to make you afraid."

"It should have been you. Jack, you waited for so long. I tortured you."

"You did." Jack laughed sadly. "But it was divine torture."

"No. It was cruel. All through college, in that terrible dorm room. All the cock teasing. I should have been punished."

"I understood your mindset back then."

"And when I dated Sharon. How cruel was that?"

"You thought you had to marry. I understood that as well."

"I don't deserve a friend like you. I've abused you horribly. How can you even stand the sight of me?"

Jack touched Mark's jaw and urged him back. Mark met Jack's watery eyes. "Believe me, Mark. I can stand the sight of you."

Mark connected their mouths and deepened the kiss until his skin danced with chills. He didn't want to stop. He wanted to kiss Jack all night. But it was getting late and there were two other men involved in this scenario.

Mark parted softly from the kiss. "What do we do now, love?"

"I wish I had the answer to that question." Jack dug his hand through Mark's hair.

"Cheat? Go behind their backs?"

"I hate that option."

"They would never let us have sex."

"I don't know." Jack sighed tiredly.

"Steve may, if he was involved." Mark immediately thought of the foursome, he, Steve, Keith, and Carl having sex together. "Would Adam? If it was a group thing?"

"I have no idea. I think if Adam knew it was just a way for us to have sex, he wouldn't be too keen."

"No. Of course not." Mark caressed Jack's hair. "Do you love him?"

"Yes. I do."

"You don't sound convincing."

Jack lowered his eyes. "It's hard for me to allow that deep feeling to flow again, Mark."

"Because of me."

"Yes." Jack met his eyes. "Because of you. I felt I could never love anyone the way I loved, still love, you. And though it's unfair to Adam, I don't think anyone else will ever capture that piece of me."

"Oh, baby," Mark moaned. "I'm such an idiot. I hate myself for the nightmare I've made. I can't make a goddamn good decision if my life depended on it."

Jack caressed his face. "You do the best you can at the time you make a decision. No one's perfect."

131

"But I always make such a cock-up of everything. I'm a complete failure."

"Stop it. You're not. I hate it when you say those things about yourself."

"Look at me." Mark gestured to his position on top of Jack. "You don't think this night is a complete nightmare?"

"Oh, hell no." Jack kissed Mark again.

"I want to make love to you."

"We'll have to arrange it."

"I hate the cheating. I have to tell Steve."

"Oh, that'll go over big."

"I can't do it behind his back. Seriously. I can't. I'll crack up. I'm not good at that kind of thing."

"You do what you think is best." Jack checked his watch. "Adam will be wondering where I am."

"What did you tell him?" Mark struggled to climb back to the driver's seat.

"That you needed legal advice on a shoot."

"Oh. Sorry."

"Don't worry. I told you, let me handle Adam."

Mark managed to plop back into the driver's side. Jack picked up the envelope and pulled the photo out again.

To see it with him, Mark leaned on Jack's shoulder. "It is lovely."

"It is."

"Look at your hair. It was very long."

"Mine?" Jack laughed.

"I look like a girl."

"I'm afraid you do, Mark."

"Want me to make a copy?"

"Yes. Please." Jack slid it back inside.

"Where's your car?"

"Behind the restaurant."

"I'll drive you."

Once Mark started the car, Jack held his hand tightly.

As Mark drove, he knew this was the way it should be. He and Jack. It felt right.

Mark was completely drained. He figured Steve could hear him come into the kitchen from the garage. A minute later, Steve appeared in the room.

"Hiya." Mark tried to smile.

Steve deliberately looked at the clock on the kitchen wall. It was ten thirty. "What's that?"

Mark hid the envelope behind his back.

Like lightning Steve reached around Mark and tugged the folder from his hand. "You stink like booze."

Mark bit his lip, waiting for Steve to pull out the photo. "What the fuck?" Steve stared at it in confusion. "You and Jack? When was this taken?"

"1993." Mark took off his shoes.

Steve met his eyes. "Then you and he did screw around?"

"No. We didn't." Mark left the room to head upstairs.

Steve followed him. "Who did you have a drink with?"

"Here comes the twenty questions." Mark unraveled his tie. While he was standing in the walk-in closet, he removed his clothing, surprised Steve wasn't attached to him, badgering him.

When he was down to his briefs, Mark stepped out of the closet. Steve was sitting on their bed, staring at the photograph. In a deep depression for so many reasons, Mark headed to the bathroom to wash up and relieve himself. Once he had brushed his teeth and gargled to get rid of the alcohol taste and scent, he emerged. Steve was still in the same position.

Mark dropped down on the bed next to him.

"Christ, you were so beautiful. How old were you?"

"Twenty-one."

"Jesus. Look at your hair."

"It was long." Mark rested on Steve's shoulder, staring at it.

"Jack must have been so in love with you."

"Yes, he was." *And still is.*

"Did this have to do with that book you once posed for?"

"Yes. Janis Campbell was the photographer. She was at the shoot tonight."

"Ah." Steve nodded, as if he got the information he needed. "I'm going to buy that book. I know Larsen has a copy but I didn't think it was right to ask to see it."

"Why not? He'd show it to you."

"I'll order my own copy." Steve rose up, propping the photo up against the mirror on their dresser. "Did it go all right?"

"Yes. It was fine. I'm shattered, love. I have to sleep." Mark crawled under the sheet.

Steve washed up and stripped before he came to bed. He took a long look at the photograph prior to shutting off the light. Mark noticed his erection and dragged his briefs down his legs, pushing them out of the bed and onto the floor.

Before Steve even asked, Mark rolled to his stomach and spread his legs. He closed his eyes and pressed into the pillows, listening as Steve prepared himself. With one arm, Steve raised Mark's hips up off the bed, sliding inside Mark with a hiss of a breath.

"Yes. Take me, love. Take what's yours." Mark imagined Steve envisioning screwing the twenty-one-year-old Mark Richfield, that long-haired seraph who could make any man kneel before him.

For a split second Mark pretended Jack was inside him. Even through his weariness, that thought lit him up. As his cock engorged with his taboo thoughts, he whispered, "Hold me, Steven." Instantly Steve gripped his cock and worked it.

The rush running through him from visions of Jack taking his ass, kissing him and the image of them in that photo, Mark came, shivering down to his toes.

Steve banged his ass as he did, fucking him with wild abandon. While he drove in deep, Steve sealed their bodies together as he ejaculated, whimpering and grunting.

Not moving, Mark deliberately savored the throbbing inside him. "Yes...oh, yes." When Steve pulled out, Mark felt the void with sadness.

As he felt Steve shift on the bed, Mark sat back on his heels while Steve went to wash up. Mark first stared down at the come spattered on the sheets before twisting back to see that photo now displayed ominously. *You must feel very confident in our love, Steven, to place that photo there.*

"And so you should be." Mark wiped at the last drop of come beading on the tip of his cock.

Steve appeared with a wet washcloth and dabbed at the sheet. "I thought you would be too tired to come."

"I was. But it felt so damn good."

After scrubbing at the spot, Steve admitted, "I was thinking of you as a twenty-year-old."

"I figured." Mark smiled wryly at him.

"You sleep on the wet spot, hot stuff."

Mark dropped down on it. "At least it's cool."

When Steve returned from the bathroom, he cuddled around Mark from behind, cupping his hand over his genitals. "I love you, Mark Antonious."

"I love you too, Steven Jay."

Steve kissed him between the shoulder blades so Mark

wriggled against him affectionately.

As the weariness sought to claim him, Mark wondered if Steve would understand. He knew he would have a much easier time with it than Jack would with Adam.

Chapter Twelve

At work the next day Mark passed by Steve's office, peeking in. About to keep going when he found him busy on his computer, Mark backtracked when Steve called his name. "Mark?"

"Yes, my sweet?" Entering his office, Mark stood behind Steve's chair. Once he was able to see the computer screen he realized Steve was surfing the Amazon website. "Oh. Yes, I wanted to see what books Janis has published since I did my photo shoot with her."

"It's this one, right?" Steve pointed to the cover photo of the book on screen.

"Yes."

Steve clicked "add to cart". "There. Perfect. How many shots do you have in it?"

"Uh, three? No, four? I forget. Once was just my torso, if I remember right. I was embracing another man, or he was embracing me. Christ, it's been so long ago, I can hardly recall." Mark knelt down beside him. "Click on her name and let me see her collection."

In response, Steve moved the mouse and brought up a list of all her books.

"Look at that," Mark exclaimed at the sight of naked men on the book covers. "Yum, yum."

"Want it?"

"We shouldn't drool over nude photographs, should we? Is that sad?" Mark bit his lip. "Click on 'search inside this book'."

Both he and Steve groaned in harmony at the sight of an incredibly fit naked male body.

"How hot is that?" Steve rubbed his crotch.

"Bloody hell. She's amazing." Mark's cock twitched at the black-and-white nude shots of unbelievably handsome men. "We shouldn't."

"So, just the one with you in it?" Steve asked.

"Yes. I'd be doing nothing but staring at those books all night."

"Great foreplay."

"I've got my hunk." Mark stroked Steve's leg.

"Wow. That's flattering. You mean it?"

"Are you kidding me?" Mark rose up and looked at the office door. He didn't like anyone seeing them playing during work time but the staff tolerated their flirting. Mark and Steve even enjoyed some good-natured teasing about it. Even so, Mark liked to keep it as professional as he could during office hours.

"I don't know, Mark. Sometimes I get the feeling you've gone off me."

"Never." Mark grabbed Steve's head and kissed it quickly.

"Do...do you think I'm still attractive? I mean, after seeing Carl and Keith naked?"

"God, yes. Don't worry." Mark shook his head at the absurdity.

"I just feel it's me getting off on you, and you're not really a part of the sex."

Mark felt crushed. "That's not true."

"It sometimes is. I mean, I just fuck you and you just take it."

"We shouldn't have this conversation here." Mark backed around Steve's desk in paranoia. Perhaps this was going too deep for where they were at the moment.

"But am I right?"

"I love getting it in the end, love. I can't get enough of it."

"Are you sure?" Steve stood, closing the gap between them.

If Steve feels this way, how on earth am I going to ask him for free rein to have sex with Jack?

"Yes. I've been slightly more tired than normal. I feel as if I'm working two jobs. And the heat, love, the heat and the exertion from the run, it wears me out."

"Okay. As long as it's not me. I just want to turn you on as much as you turn me on." Steve touched Mark's fingers delicately.

"You do. Oh, Officer Miller, you sexy stud, you do." Mark brought Steve's hand to his crotch and pressed his hard-on into it.

"Oh yes!" Steve lit up.

"But we're at work, love."

"Thank you, Mark."

"Thank you?" Mark released Steve's hand.

"Yes. I suppose everyone needs reassurance every now and then."

"Yes, of course. I should tell you more often what I think. I just get sidetracked. Too much on me mind." Mark smiled, tapping his own head. "Always in a muddle."

Steve sat down at his desk again. "Right. One book."

"One book." Mark retreated from his office. "I've got some calls to make."

"Okay. Catch you later."

As he walked down the corridor, Mark's warm smile fell from his face. *I'm such a flamin' idiot.*

139

After making appointments for next week for advertising deals, Mark checked his mobile phone's voicemail. Arnold had left a message reminding him of yet another appointment that evening. It was overwhelming him. Three nights in a row he had shoots. Mark began to think this wasn't just some light dabbling in modeling. It was becoming a full-time job. What had seemed like a good idea originally, he slightly resented now.

"I can't think straight." Mark rested his head on his hands to take a mini break. He closed his eyes. He couldn't prioritize his tasks and it was giving him a headache. The phone on his desk rang. "Mark Richfield, can I help you?"

"Mark."

At the sound of Jack's voice, Mark melted. "Hello, Jackie-blue," he whispered.

"I just called to see how you were. Last night was pretty crazy."

"I'm a mess as usual. I keep torturing myself. I must love the pain." Mark tried to sound light, but Jack knew him too well to fake it.

"You always were a masochist. Are you that way in bed?"

"Yes, I'm afraid so." Mark smiled sadly.

"Oooh, that makes my skin tingle."

"I'm a bottom. Always will be, love."

"And what a bottom it is." Jack smiled.

Mark and Jack had flirted this way in the past, but it was different now. Mark wanted to fulfill Jack's fantasy this time. He was afraid, but not for the same reasons.

"I..." Mark choked back his emotions. "I have visions of you and Steve with me. Of pleasing you both."

"Naughty boy."

"Yes. I'm terrible."

"Do you think of us both on you at the same time?"

"Sometimes." Mark checked the hallway outside his office

door.

"Christ, just thinking about screwing you gets me insane. You have any idea how many times I've done it in my dreams?"

"I don't want you to dream it anymore, love. I want you in me."

"*Ohhh,*" Jack moaned sensually.

"How? That's all I want to know. How can we do it?"

"Did you talk to Steve?"

"I couldn't. Just an hour ago he mentioned he was feeling slightly insecure with me. Jack, I don't intentionally make my men feel that way. Why do they always end up nervous about me?"

"You're too pretty. Both Steve and I know how many offers you get."

Mark rubbed his face in agony. "I go with no one."

"I know," Jack whispered.

"Jackie..." Mark sighed. When he looked up, Steve was standing in the doorway. "Shite."

"What's wrong?" Jack asked.

Mark didn't know what to do. Should he lie? Tell Steve it was Jack? Hang up?

"Mark?" Jack inquired, "Are you still there?"

"Steven, Jack's on the line," Mark said for both of their sakes.

"Yeah? Does he want us to get together with him and Adam?" Steve sat in the supple leather chair across from Mark's desk.

"Uh, Jackie, Steve asked if you wanted us to get together again?"

"I want to suck your cock, Richfield."

"Oh!" Mark gulped. "Yes. Uh."

Steve leaned across the desk. "What did he say?"

141

"He...he..." Mark broke out in a sweat.

Jack breathed seductively, "I want to suck you until you scream with orgasm, then screw you up the ass, hard."

"He...he..." Mark pointed to the phone nervously.

"He what?" Steve tilted his head. "Do they want to come by our place? Or go out somewhere? What about Chinese food?"

"Jackie?" Mark asked timidly. "Steve wondered if you wanted to come to our place or go out for Chinese food?" He never took his gaze off his lover, and prayed Steve couldn't hear Jack from over the line.

"I want to taste your come."

Mark shivered at the thought. "He said Chinese is fine," he relayed to Steve, trying to keep his features calm.

"Good. We can't tonight because you have a shoot. How about tomorrow?" Steve asked.

"Jack?" Mark cleared his throat. "Steven wants to know if tomorrow is good for you and Adam?"

"I'm going to fuck you so hard you'll take me balls deep."

"Ah!" Mark squeaked at the image. "Yes. Saturday is fine."

"What the hell is he saying to you?" Steve made a move to listen.

"Nothing. So, Jackie...Saturday? We'll call you with the reservations?"

"See me tonight. Call me when you can."

"Yes. Fine. Bye." Mark hung up, his hand shaking as he set the phone back in its cradle.

"That was fucking weird." Steve reclined in the chair. "What was going on?"

"Nothing. Shall we go?" Mark shut down his computer.

"Mark?"

142

At the terse tone, Mark peered at Steve from under his long hair.

"What's going on with you and Jack?" Steve enunciated slowly.

"Why do you think something's going on?" Mark shuffled a few papers on his desk.

"You think I'm stupid? I was a cop for ten years, sweetie."

Mark deflated at the comment, stood and walked around Steve to shut his office door. Once they were in private Mark sat on Steve's lap and snuggled with him. "You know I love you?"

"Uh huh."

"That I'm so mad for you I'd do anything to please you?"

"Oh no."

"What?"

"You want to screw Larsen."

Mark stifled a choke in his throat.

"So? Do I get to play too, or are just the two of you finally having sex after twenty years?"

"You…you…" Mark blinked in astonishment.

"Well? Mark, that photo…come on. Jack was so fucking in love with you. You can tell by the expression on his face. And you!" Steve whistled. "You look like a goddamn angel. You and that hair. He'd be a robot not to want to screw you."

"I love you." Mark kissed his face. "You are the most amazing boyfriend any man could have."

"And you, Mr. Richfield, are high maintenance. High motherfucking maintenance!" Steve laughed, then asked, "What does Adam say?"

"Er…" Mark hid his face in Steve's neck.

"Oh. I get it. He has no idea."

"I'm not sure. Jack said to let him deal with Adam."

"Christ, what am I supposed to do? If I say no, the two of

you will cheat on me. If I say yes, that gives you carte blanche to screw Jack to your heart's content."

"No. No, Steven. You will be part of it."

"Yeah, Jack will love that." Steve rolled his eyes.

"Tough. He has me with you, or he doesn't have me."

Steve leaned back to see Mark's eyes. "You mean it?"

"I do."

"I wouldn't mind fucking Larsen. I offered a three-way before with him. Remember?"

Mark smiled, licking Steve's cheek the way Mark had done to Jack in the photo.

"I want that on film." Steve laughed. "You call that photographer and you get one of us doing that."

"She'd love it." Mark nestled into Steve's face excitedly.

"Good."

"I adore you, Officer Miller."

"Mr. Richfield," Steve sighed heavily, "you are a handful."

"Not half!" Mark grabbed Steve's hand and cupped it over his erection.

"Make that two hands." Steve smiled sweetly, kissing him.

Anxious about yet another shoot at another location, Mark was tired. He wanted to rest after a very long week and stressful day.

As he drove to the new address Arnold had given him, which he'd scribbled on a notepaper, Mark recalled the conversation with Steve about Jack.

Tiny ripples of pleasure washed over him whenever he thought of Steve's generosity. Mark adored Steve for understanding. *There is no way Jack is going to convince Adam. No way.*

Not finding the address easily, Mark pulled over after

circling the same block twice, and took out his phone. He called Arnold's number first and got his voicemail. After saying, "Jesus Christ," under his breath, he dialed the contact directly. "Yes, hello. My name is Mark Richfield and I'm scheduled for a photo shoot with you. I just can't seem to find you."

"Where are you?"

Mark leaned closer to the windshield and made out the nearby street sign. The evening was cooling off as clouds moved east from the sea. "Coldwater Canyon just north of Burbank."

"Park. You're just about at our location. Do you see the Bistro Garden?"

"I do."

"It's the apartment house just beyond it."

"Apartment house?" Mark didn't like the sound of that.

"3B. See ya soon." The line disconnected.

"What the fuck?" After gazing at the mobile phone in annoyance, Mark parked closer to the curb and shut off the engine. Something about this situation sent the hairs rising on the back of his neck, though he had no idea why.

Before he left the car Mark made sure he placed his phone in his pocket. He locked up the car, buttoned his suit jacket and walked down the street. He didn't like the look of the place. "What the bloody hell? An apartment house? No, this can't be right." Again, trying to get verification or maybe just reassurance, Mark tried Arnold's cell phone number this time. Again all he reached was his voicemail. The phone back in his pocket, Mark took a good look at the building, craning his neck at its nine floors and slightly put off by the rundown appearance.

"Shite." It didn't matter that everything in his gut was telling him to skip it. He had a sense of responsibility to his friends and his job. Arnold hadn't steered him wrong up to now.

Mark cursed under his breath as he buzzed apartment 3B.

145

A humming noise and the sound of metal met his ear. He tried the door. It was unlocked. The hallway stunk. "Uh oh, no, this is no good." He retreated, standing by the front door. *Don't be silly. What's wrong with you, you sissy! What are you a girl?*

Once the internal chiding relented, he inhaled for strength and, not seeing an elevator, he walked up the dank hot flight of dirty steps to the third floor. Cat urine odor found his nostrils. He cringed.

He found the correct apartment and paused to collect himself. With all his might he was trying not to be intimidated. The hall was filthy. Paint peeled like sunburned skin from the walls. Gang graffiti marked the back wall—unsuccessfully wiped clean, it was a smeared blue mass of lines. There was noise from other units, loud televisions, or maybe shouting, Mark didn't know which. Against all his better judgment, he rapped on the door lightly.

A moment later a man with a shaven head answered the door. He was covered in tattoos up both arms like sleeves and wore a worn faded T-shirt and blue jeans.

Shit. Mark knew he was in trouble, but he kept up his professionalism and was determined to get through this shoot. *Like a man.* "Uh, hi." He cleared his throat. "Am I in the right place?"

"Yeah." The tattooed man opened the door and looked him up and down. "Come in."

The interior of the apartment reeked of cigarette smoke and rotten garbage. A tatty sofa, a coffee table covered in beer bottles and full ashtrays, and a television set were the contents of the front room.

"This is where the shoot is for Sunspec Corporation?" Mark asked.

"I contract out. Freelancing. I do work for a lot of different clients. This way."

Mark was directed to another room. It was a makeshift

studio with a couple of spotlights pointing in opposing directions, a painter's drop cloth on the floor, a large standing fan, and a backdrop of a beach tacked to the back wall. Two men were already inside, smoking cigarettes, looking as rough as the guy who met him at the door.

At the cloud of smoke Mark waved his hand in front of his face and coughed.

"What's the matter?" the first man asked.

"I don't smoke." Mark squinted his eyes in the haze.

"Put your cigarettes out, boys. The man don't like it."

It was sarcastic and mean-spirited. Mark wanted to leave. *This can't be good.* "Look, maybe I'm not the right model for this one."

"No. You're perfect. Here. Try these on." The tattooed man handed Mark a pair of sunglasses.

The two other men in the room leered at him while Mark slipped the glasses on.

"Perfect. Take off your suit."

"What?" Mark shivered. "I don't think so, mate."

"I need you to look like you're on a beach, *mate.* Not your pants. Just your top half."

His instinct told him to get the hell out of there. Mark knew all he needed to do was say "no thank you" and leave. But a force in him kept him from doing it. He felt obligated. A sense of duty. Or was it to prove he was a real man and not an androgynous weakling?

With resignation, Mark tossed his jacket on a high stool and unknotted his necktie, trying to get through this quickly. When he peeled back his shirt, he glanced at the men. All three were staring.

"Bloody, bloody hell," he mumbled to himself. Rid of his top half of clothing, Mark crossed his arms over his naked chest and asked, "Where do you want me?"

A wicked chuckle wafted through the stinky air. Mark ignored it.

"Over there," the tattooed man pointed to the fake backdrop of the beach photo. The cheap plastic image couldn't be any tackier.

Mark stood in front of it while the first man, who never introduced himself or his slimy friends, put on the fan, blowing back Mark's hair.

Though it took an effort, Mark tried not to be distracted by the odd audience. He adjusted the glasses and kept repeating in his head, *Just take the bloody photos and let me get out of here.*

Tattoo man leaned down to peer through the lens of a camera on a tripod. "Nice. Look left."

Mark did, struggling to get through this horrible session.

The camera whirred. "Look right."

Fine. Yes, what-fucking-ever.

"Great. Man, you're amazing. Look straight ahead."

When Mark did, the fan blew his hair across his face. One of the other men jumped to his feet and brushed it back for him. Mark forced a "thank you" out of his closed throat.

"My pleasure." The man grinned at Mark, showing off a chipped tooth.

Oh, Christ. Shoot me.

"Wow. You're really hot," Tattoo-man said as the shutter clicked several times. "Take another pair of sunglasses."

Mark noticed a large selection set out on a folding table and approached it. "Does it matter which?"

"No."

"Are you British?" the third man asked.

In an effort to not appear terrified, Mark didn't meet his eyes, sorting through the mess of glasses. He had no doubt the scary man had a mug shot and a police record. "No." He exchanged the pair he was wearing for another. "Is this all right?"

"Perfect." The first man continued to stand by the camera.

"He sounds British to me. Doesn't he sound British to you guys? You sure you're not from England?"

About to explode, Mark ground his jaw. "My mother is."

"Ah, see. I can hear it." Mug-shot-man pointed to his ear proudly.

"Okay, Mark. Same thing. Left, right, and forward."

If this idiot thinks I'm going to do this with five hundred pairs of fucking sunglasses, he's mad.

Obediently, Mark moved back to his spot in front of the backdrop, going through the same series of poses. When Mark faced forward, the fan nailed him again. Before the other man touched him, Mark tried to tame his own hair. It didn't work.

"No. No. I'm the guy who does that."

Mug-shot-man stunk of nicotine. He fussed over Mark's hair, touching it gently, combing it back from his face. "Man, you models are so nice looking."

In frustration at being helpless to leave, to get away from these brutes, Mark began grinding his jaw. He couldn't bear it for much longer.

"Randy, he's the best-looking guy you've had here so far for these glasses. Isn't he?" After addressing Tattoo-man, Mug-shot-man grinned wickedly.

"He's amazing. Step aside, Joe." Randy leaned back down to his camera lens.

After smoothing his callused fingers over Mark's neck and shoulders, Joe moved back to his viewing spot against the wall.

"I can't stay much longer." Mark licked his dry lips. "I assume this will wrap it up?"

"What's the rush? I told Newhouse an hour. It's been fifteen minutes," Randy said.

Mark chided himself to be patient and professional. "Yes.

All right."

A low snickering laugh made his skin crawl. *If I were Jack or Steve, I'd leave. I'd say "fuck you, asshole" and leave. I am weak. I'm a fucking sissy, just like my father said I was.*

"Go get another pair. Make it the aviators. You need to choose a totally different pair." Randy pointed to the chaotic folding table once again.

Mark returned to the mess of sunglasses reluctantly. When he peered behind him, Randy had set up a stool and was bouncing a beach ball prop.

A new pair of sunglasses on his face, Mark waited for instructions.

"No. Don't like those." Randy walked to the table. "Come here."

Once he approached the table, Mark took the glasses off his face and set them down while Randy began offering his selections. As Mark reached to place them on himself, Randy said, "Oblige me."

"Oblige you? What does that bloody mean?"

"Don't you love his accent?" Joe gushed.

"It means, let me do it." Randy's tone grew more unfriendly.

Mark folded his arms impatiently while Randy pulled sunglasses on and off his head.

"For fuck sake!" Mark moaned. "Decide. I don't have all night." The calm expression on Randy's face fell. Mark regretted his tone instantly. "Look, I'm sorry. It's been a long week."

When Randy dug his hand into Mark's hair, Mark tensed up. "Been a long week for all of us, darling."

"All right. Just get on with it." Mark clenched his teeth and leaned away from the touch.

"Is he being nasty, Randy?" Joe stood.

"You know how these conceited pretty boys are." Randy tightened his grip on Mark's hair.

Mark flinched and tried to see the other two men. They were approaching him. *Fuck.*

"Look, mates, I didn't mean anything by it. I'm just weary. Can we finish the shoot?" The heat of someone standing directly behind him mingled with his naked skin. Mark couldn't turn to look because Randy still had his hair in a hold. He reached up, touching Randy's fingers lightly. "Let go. You're beginning to hurt me."

Mark's face was dragged closer to Randy's. "Am I?"

"Oy! That's enough." Mark pressed his hands against Randy's chest to get away.

Someone caressed Mark's bottom through his slacks.

"Hey!" Mark struggled to shove Randy away so he could turn around. "What the hell's going on here? Let go!" Mark twisted out of Randy's grip. When he raised his jaw, the three men were looking at him like he was raw meat and they were a pack of hungry wolves.

"I've finished here." Mark tried to push past them to his clothing.

"No. You're not." Randy smirked.

"I don't know what you're on about. I came here for a photo shoot and obviously you men have something else in mind. The answer is no. Get out of my way."

"Not so fast. I'm not done yet."

"I'm sorry to tell you, you are." Mark slammed into Randy with his shoulder, managing to get by. He nearly reached his shirt when someone grabbed him.

"Oy!" Mark admonished him, gripping the arms that surrounded him from the rear. "What do you think you're doing? You know damn well this is ridiculous. Do you really think you can get away with something?"

Joe squeezed him from behind, inhaling his skin. "Oh, Christ, he smells good."

Mark shouted, "Let go of me! I demand you release me!" His skin broke out in chills. He was way over his head. Steve's warning rang in his ears. He never gave Steve the location of the shoot. He was screwed.

"Don't you just love his accent?" Joe wrapped his hands tighter around Mark's torso, trapping Mark's arms.

"I do." Randy cupped Mark's jaw. "I love everything about him."

"What do you want?" Mark panted for breath. "Why won't you leave me alone?"

The third man reached out his hand, touching Mark's crotch. Mark spun his hips away from the contact.

"Bet he's hung like a horse."

Mark roared in fury, trying to break the hold. Randy cupped his hand over Mark's mouth and said, "You better shut up."

His brain going haywire, Mark couldn't think any longer. *I deserve this. Isn't this the perfect end to my life? I've inflicted so much pain on people, this is my just desserts.*

He was very sure he was not going to get out of this alive.

"Be quiet."

Mark nodded. The hand was lowered from his mouth slowly.

"What do you want?" Mark was hyperventilating.

Taking his sweet time, Randy had a good look at Mark from head to toe. "Damn, you're pretty."

"Are you planning on raping me?" Mark figured he'd get it out there on the table.

"I hadn't originally. But it is a thought."

"And?" Mark tried to keep his voice down. "You think I'll do nothing? I won't go to the police?"

"Not if you enjoy it." Joe sniffed Mark's hair from behind.

"I won't enjoy it." Mark ground his jaw.

"How do you know?" Randy stroked Mark's cheek.

"How do I know?" Mark laughed, near hysteria.

"Three big, beefy men? All servicing you?" The third man rubbed his hand over Mark's zipper. "Could be fun."

"Oh, God... Please. Leave me alone." Mark cringed.

"See, Dave?" Randy grinned. "You're already turnin' him on."

Sure he was going completely mad, Mark screamed, "Leave me the fuck alone!"

One of the men smacked him hard and threw him down onto the floor. He went crashing into the wall and rolled to his back, touching his jaw. When he looked up, the three men were standing over him. In fear Mark moved to the corner of the room, met each of their eyes and shivered in terror. "No. Whatever you're thinking, the answer is no."

They laughed, glancing at each other.

Chapter Thirteen

Steve checked the time. He sighed in annoyance, and flipped the channels on the television dully, not finding anything worthwhile to watch. Out of boredom, he grabbed the phone and dialed Mark's mobile phone number. It rang for a while until the service finally picked up. "You still on the shoot? Man, why do those things take so long? Call me." He hung up. "Shit, Richfield. I don't like you being gone every night."

Steve missed him. Nights and weekends used to be theirs to enjoy. Not anymore.

He hated television so he shut the thing off. Steve rubbed his face and wanted to go to bed. He just wouldn't be able to sleep without Mark in it with him.

"Mark!" he moaned. "Come home."

"Who are you calling?" Adam asked Jack as they stood in the kitchen together.

"Mark." Jack put his cell phone to his ear.

"What for?"

"He wanted to get together with us this Saturday night for Chinese food." Jack got Mark's voicemail. "Mark, it's Jack. Call me." He hung up and tried his home number.

"Which Chinese restaurant?" Adam asked.

"I don't know."

"Hello?"

"Steve?"

"Yeah, Jack?"

"Yes. Uh, I was just calling back to see when and where you wanted to go Saturday."

"I have to check with Mark."

"Where is he?"

"At another photo shoot. Jack, I don't like it. I swear it freaks me out he's out there alone at night posing for strangers."

A flutter of worry washed over Jack's skin. "Does he tell you where he is?"

"No. We had an argument about it. He was upset I was treating him like a woman."

"Yes. That's Mark's pet-peeve."

"I know it's crazy, but he's so fucking pretty I get paranoid someone will want to hurt him if he says no."

A second rush of nerves washed over Jack's body. "What time is he expected back?"

"Fuck. I never know. Last night he didn't get home 'til ten thirty. And he had gone out for drinks. I didn't push him but I assumed it was with that photographer, Janis Campbell."

A feeling of guilt rushed over Jack. Adam stood next to him, listening, staring at him. "Yes. That's the woman who took his picture for that book of male nudes."

"She gave him a photo of you guys together. You should see it. It's amazing."

Jack didn't want to say he'd already seen it and get both he and Mark into hot water. "Oh?"

"Mark is licking your face. Christ, he was so pretty."

"Yes." Jack's expression was a mask while Adam eavesdropped.

"He told me you two want to connect. I'm okay with that, Jack…as long as I can play too."

Shocked, Jack stifled a choke of awe in his throat. "Oh, well, we'll have to talk about that some other time."

"Adam listening?"

"Uh, yes. So, you have no idea where Mark is?"

"No. I'm worried sick."

Jack checked the time. It was nearing ten. "I tried his cell phone."

"Me too. He shuts it off during the sessions."

"What do you want me to do?"

"I don't know. I suppose you coming here and both of us worrying isn't going to accomplish anything."

"You really have no inkling where he is?"

"No."

Jack ran his hand through his hair nervously. "Shit."

"I'm probably worried for nothing."

"Yes. Probably."

"I'll tell Mark to call you when he gets in."

"Please do. To at least let me know he's okay."

"Cool. Thanks, Jack."

Jack hung up and found Adam's suspicious glare. "Mark's at a photo shoot and Steve's worried."

"Why?"

"Because he knows Mark's an easy target, that's why." Jack set the phone down and rubbed his face tiredly, thinking of Steve allowing them to have sex with Mark together. It was blowing his mind.

"Don't worry about Mark." Adam walked away. "He can take care of himself."

When he was left alone, Jack shook his head. "Not the Mark I know."

With his back against the wall, Mark held out his hand in a gesture to stop. "Look. This is absurd." He caught his breath. "I came here for a photo shoot and you've taken enough pictures. Now it's time for me to go."

As he rose to his feet, he was shoved back down.

"What!" Mark cried. "Leave me alone! Do you get that I'm not interested? Huh?"

"He says he's not interested in us, Randy." Joe crossed his arms. "I guess we're not his type."

"No. I suppose pretty boys like him like other pretty boys." Joe pulled a cigarette out of his pack. "Sorry, gotta smoke, man."

"Fine. Whatever." Mark tried to stand again, sliding against the wall. "Randy." He spoke softly. "I assume you're a businessman."

Randy smirked.

"And you wouldn't want any bad reputation preventing you from acquiring more business." Mark pushed his hair back from his eyes. He was glistening with sweat. "So, I won't say a word to Arnold Newhouse about this. Okay?"

"Sure." Randy appeared to be humoring him.

"Good. I have to go." Mark made a move to pass them and was shoved back to the wall again. "Stop doing that." He pointed a warning finger. "Why can't I leave?"

Joe turned to Randy and asked sarcastically, "Gee, Randy? Why can't the pretty boy just go?"

"I don't know, Joe. Do you, Dave?"

Mark sank down against the plasterboard and covered his face in anguish. He blinked back tears from frustration and it brought on callous laughter.

"He's crying," Dave whined. "You boys made him cry."

"Oh, poor baby." Joe crouched down and petted Mark's

hair.

Mark hissed like a cornered cat and swatted his hand away. "Leave me alone."

"I'll enjoy taming you." Joe reached for Mark's leg.

Mark curled up in a ball to get away from him. "Don't fucking touch me."

"You don't talk to me like that, lady."

"Lady?" Mark snapped. "Who you calling a bloody lady?"

"You!" Joe grabbed Mark's slacks and tugged at them.

Mark kicked at him to get him off. The other two jumped in, wrestling with Mark's arms to allow Joe to drag his slacks down his legs.

"No!" Mark roared, tensing his body and clamping his legs tightly together.

"Behave, pretty lady, or we'll get rough on you." Joe caressed Mark's hair lovingly.

His chest heaving with fear, Mark watched in agony as his slacks were slowly torn from his body. "Oh, Christ, oh, bloody Christ." He cringed. "Don't. I'm begging you. Don't."

His trousers were tossed aside.

"Next?" Joe laughed, the cigarette hanging from his lips. He dug his fingers into Mark's briefs.

"Please," Mark cried, struggling with the other two who held him. "What did I do to you? Why are you doing this?"

"Get ready, fellas." Joe laughed as he dragged Mark's briefs down his thighs. "Oh, yes. Jackpot."

Mark bucked his body to get away, clenching his eyes closed and his jaw shut. "Please," he begged, "I won't tell anyone. Please."

"Get the camera, Randy."

"No! No!" Mark opened his eyes instantly. "What are you doing?"

"Oh, pretty lady..." Joe unzipped his jeans. "Time for some fun."

"No! Get the fuck away from me." Mark began screaming, "Help! Help!"

A rag filled his mouth and he choked. While Randy crouched down with the camera, Joe and Dave twisted Mark to his belly on the floor. In shock, shaking his head in denial, Mark wanted to die. If this happened, he'd never be able to survive it.

He closed his eyes, hoping they would kill him when they were through. In what felt as if time had stopped, he heard only his own heartbeat and blasting respirations through his nostrils.

Suddenly there came a loud cracking noise and shouting. Mark assumed he must be hallucinating and blocked it out, trying to believe he was asleep and having a nightmare. He cringed and prayed.

"Police! Get on the floor! Get on the floor! NOW!"

Mark lay still, terrified to look. When he dared, a dozen men in black uniforms and helmets with semi-automatic firearms had flooded the room. Randy, Joe and Dave were laid out flat and handcuffed. Mark shivered, terrified to move.

"Bedroom clear!"

"Bathroom clear!"

"The place is clear, Sarge."

"Good. What the hell do we have here?"

"Porno?"

"I don't think so." A large male in black with white chevrons on his shoulder and the letters SWAT on his chest crouched down next to Mark. The sergeant removed the gag from his mouth.

Mark looked up at the sergeant's face. "Help me."

"Jesus H. Christ. What the hell is going on here?" The sergeant stood, turning around. "Take those three assholes downstairs and book them for assault."

"Right, Sarge."

Mark shivered as Randy, Joe and Dave were roughly yanked to their feet and escorted out of the room, shouting "We didn't do nuthin'!" in protest.

"Oh, God…" Mark moaned.

The sergeant knelt down beside him again. "All right. You're safe now."

The sergeant helped Mark sit up. Behind the handsome cop Mark could hear the three fiends yelling about their innocence. He couldn't stop shivering in strong tremors.

The sergeant held onto his shoulder tightly. The man barked orders at the other uniformed men in the room. "Get a medic unit out here."

"Got it, Sarge."

"You okay?" The big cop took off his helmet and goggles, setting them aside.

Mark's teeth chattered. "Yes. I think so."

"I'm Sergeant Billy Sharpe. You're safe now. Where's your clothing?"

Mark made a movement to point somewhere in the room. He was disoriented.

"Okay? You sit still. Will you be okay while I look?"

"Yes. Thank you." Mark noticed one other man with a black helmet and goggles in the room, the letters SWAT in white on his chest, his gun pointed upwards, glancing at him but trying not to stare.

"Here. Is this yours?"

"Yes." Mark struggled to put his briefs on.

Sgt. Sharpe assisted him gently. "All right. Calm down. You're okay."

Mark felt completely helpless. "I can't do this. I'm sorry."

"I'm here." The sergeant held out Mark's trousers for him.

With one hand Mark held Sgt. Sharpe's shoulder, feeling his solid deltoid through the black shirt. It made him calmer. "Thank you."

"No problem." Sgt. Sharpe zipped them for Mark, buttoning the top. "Here's your shirt."

"Did…did you hear my shouts for help? Is that why you're here?" Mark trembled as he slid his shirt on.

"No. That was just dumb luck. We got a tip there was some illegal drugs coming from this place."

"Drugs?" Mark couldn't manage to button his shirt with his shaking fingers.

Sgt. Sharpe took over. "Yeah. I don't think it's a drug house. I guess we got some bum information."

"You're joking?" Mark gasped. "You mean, you saved me by chance?"

"We did. What's your name?"

"Mark. Mark Richfield."

The sergeant tilted his head curiously. "Why do I know that name?"

"You…you know me?" Mark tucked his shirt into his pants.

"Do you know Angel Loveday?"

"Yes. I do." Mark studied the sergeant more closely.

"He's my lover. Did he do you a favor about a year ago and come to someone's birthday party?"

"Yes. But it wasn't a birthday party. My partner saved a friend's life and he's a big fan of Angel. You're Angel's lover?"

"I am." The sergeant grinned proudly, then whispered, "Call me Billy. Okay?"

"Yes. Billy. Thank you." Mark tried to smile at him but was still very shaken up.

Behind Billy, firemen rushed in with their medical kits.

"Hello, boys," Billy greeted them. "Could you check Mr. Richfield out for me? He was in the middle of being sexually assaulted when we busted in. Is that okay, Mark?"

"Yes. Yes, of course."

"Can I call anyone for you?"

"Please." Mark found his jacket on a chair and handed Billy his phone. "Thank you."

"My pleasure, good lookin'."

"Have a seat." One of the firemen gestured to a chair. Mark dropped down on it heavily as a blood pressure cuff was wrapped around his arm.

"Who do you want me to call, Mark?" Billy looked down at Mark's phone.

"Steve. No, Jack. No. Steve."

Billy laughed softly. "How about both?"

"Yes. Thank you." Mark tried to feel safe. He kept running over the notion in his mind of the chance of the cops raiding the wrong apartment and looked up at the ceiling. "Thank you, God," he mouthed silently.

"Yes, hello, this is Sergeant Billy Sharpe with the Los Angeles Police department. Is this Jack Larsen?"

Hearing Billy say Jack's name, Mark felt relief. Jack would comfort him.

"Yes, he's doing all right. We're right on Coldwater Canyon Road."

Mark raised his arm as the cuff was removed.

"Do you need to go to the hospital?" the fireman asked.

"I don't think so."

"How far did they get in the assault?" The fireman's eyes were filled with concern.

"Not far." Mark tried to smile at him.

"You sure? No rape kit?"

"No. I am sure. Thank you."

"Hello, Steve? This is Sergeant Billy Sharpe from the LA Police Department."

As the firemen packed up their kit, they handed one of the SWAT cops a piece of paper and waved to Mark. He returned the wave in appreciation.

Billy gave Mark back his phone. "Both on the way."

"Thank you. I don't know what would have happened if you hadn't come."

After a deep exhale of breath, Billy crouched down next to Mark and held his hand tightly. "We did. That's all that counts."

"How is Angel?"

"He's very well."

"I read in the paper about that stalker." Mark shivered.

"It was horrible. I was working for the Santa Monica police back then in their property crimes division. I've only recently transferred to LA."

"My partner used to be an LA cop."

"You're shaking. Come here." Billy urged Mark out of the chair and embraced him. "You're all right."

As the adrenalin subsided, Mark felt completely spent and held him tight. "Thank you."

"Sorry about the bulky vest. I'm under here, I promise."

Mark rested his head on Billy's shoulder. "You do feel like Robocop."

"I know. Sorry."

"Don't be. You saved my life."

A few minutes later Mark heard a familiar voice. "Mark! Mark!"

At the sound of Jack, Mark spun around and raced towards the hall. Jack was bounding up the stairs. When they met, Jack wrapped his arms around him and picked Mark up off the floor.

"Baby…" Jack moaned in anguish. "What happened? What did they do to you?"

"It was horrible, Jackie. A nightmare." Mark crushed him to his chest. "I'm so glad you're here."

"Oh, my baby," Jack cried, rocking him. "Do you need to see a doctor? Should we take you to the hospital?"

"No. No, love. Nothing like that happened."

"Mark? Mark?"

"Steven!" Mark answered.

Steve raced to him and Jack and squashed Mark in his embrace. "Sweetie, are you okay?"

Billy laughed softly. "I think he's more than okay now."

With both Jack and Steve kissing him, holding him, Mark couldn't imagine feeling more loved.

"What did they do to you?" Steve asked. "I'll kill the fuckers."

"Mark," Jack whispered softly, "did they hurt you?"

"They didn't get that far. Billy showed up with an army."

"Did someone call you?" Steve asked Billy.

"We got a tip that this apartment was being used for a drug depository. It wasn't. But we did find Mark in a jam."

"You're joking." Steve inhaled in anger. "Are you telling me if you guys hadn't gotten bad information, Mark would have been…"

"Oh, my baby," Jack moaned, pressing his face into Mark's neck.

"I'm all right." Mark wrapped his arms around both his men. "I'm all right."

Billy met another cop coming in. "You got the warrant?"

"Yes, sir." He handed Billy a piece of paper.

"Okay, let's confiscate everything," Billy shouted to his men.

"You need a statement from Mark?" Steve asked, his hand caressing Mark's hair.

"Yes. I do. When he's feeling up to it."

"Can we do it here? Or in one of your patrol cars?" Steve looked behind him as an army of men entered the apartment and began taking everything out of it.

"Yes. Of course. Go down to the street level and ask one of the guys for the paperwork."

"That's Angel Loveday's partner." Mark grinned as he gestured to Billy.

"Really?" Steve smiled. "You've got great taste in men, Sarge."

"My thoughts exactly." Billy winked at Steve.

"Come on, Mark." Jack held him tight.

"Jackie, thanks for coming." Mark kissed his cheek. "What did Adam say?"

"He said he hoped you were all right." Jack walked Mark down the stairs with Steve right behind them, holding Mark's hand.

"He didn't ask to come?"

"He did. I told him he didn't have to."

"I'm sorry, love. I don't want to screw things up between you two."

"You're not."

"Hey." Steve approached one of the SWAT officers. "Your sarge needs a statement from the victim."

"Okay. Hang on." The man dug through a file in the front seat of a patrol car. He handed Steve a form. "Need a pen?"

"Yes. Please."

"Steve was an LAPD cop," Mark boasted.

"Was?" The officer smiled.

"Yeah. That job's too damn crazy." Steve took the pen

G.A. Hauser

from him.

"No kidding. I hear ya. Hey, what the heck were you doing in that apartment in the first place?" the cop asked Mark.

"Stick around. I'm taking his statement. You'll hear the whole story." Steve bent over the hood of the unmarked patrol car with the paperwork.

Mark leaned on the hot metal hood next to Steve, pulling Jack alongside him so both his men sandwiched him. "Okay. Ready, copper?"

"I am." Steve held up the pen.

"Get over here, Larsen." Mark hugged him tight. "Okay. I thought something was funny about this place the minute I realized it was an apartment building."

Mark's throat wore out from talking. Steve finished up writing, had Mark sign the bottom and handed it to Billy when he showed up on the sidewalk next to them.

The three men waited as Billy read through it. Mark had a grip on both Steve and Jack's waists, holding tight.

"You're kidding me." Billy shook his head. "Those fucking maggots."

"Let me kick their teeth in, Sarge," Steve snarled.

"Don't worry. I'll take care of it." Billy folded the paper and stuck it into his pocket. "You okay, good lookin'?"

"I am. Thank you so much, Billy."

"You got two adorable men to cuddle with now. I think you'll be just fine."

"Say hi to Angel for us." Mark smiled.

"Get over here." Billy reached out to Mark. Mark released his hold on his lovers and gave Billy a warm hug. "You watch yourself."

"I will. Thank you so much."

Steve and Jack shook Billy's hand before he left. Mark
166

smiled adoringly after him.

"You okay to drive?" Steve pushed Mark's hair back from his face.

"Yes." Mark spun around. "Jackie…"

"Yes, sweetheart."

"Can you come home with us?"

Jack checked his watch. "Adam will be waiting."

Mark brought Steve closer to be able to whisper to Jack. "Steve is okay about, you know." He kissed Steve's jaw.

"Look, Jack, I know what you guys mean to each other. I understand."

"You're an amazing man, Officer Miller." Jack shook his head in awe.

"I love the guy. What can you do?" Steve licked Mark's cheek.

"Adam. What about Adam?" Mark reached out for Jack's hands.

"Yes. Adam." Jack sighed deeply. "He may not be as open-minded."

"Come on, Jackie." Mark pouted. "Don't tell me Adam has never done anything wrong when it comes to love. He has so many beautiful men coming through his office."

Jack shrugged. "I know he was very careful because of what Turner was doing. You remember those nasty couch practices."

"Do you want us to talk to him?" Steve asked.

"God no." Jack laughed sadly. "Just don't worry about it. It'll happen." He cupped Mark's face gently. "Are you really okay?"

"Yes, my love." Mark felt like putty in his hands. Jack urged him closer, kissing him. At the passion, Mark felt the soles of his feet melt to the sidewalk. Next to them, Steve was watching, touching Mark's back, and Mark assumed he was

G.A. Hauser

doing the same to Jack.

When Jack parted from his lips, Mark felt like mush, he was so in love.

"Goodnight, Steve." Jack kissed him as well.

Mark lit up like a sparkler, watching those two alpha males connect. "Oh my God." He instantly forgot the ordeal he'd suffered and rubbed his cock on each of them in turn.

As they parted, Steve breathed, "Oh, Larsen...holy shit."

"I love you guys." Jack chuckled softly. "Hang in there."

They watched Jack walk away. He waved, turning back to them as they gazed after.

"Mark...Mark, Mark..." Steve crooned. "We have got to get that man in our bed."

"No shit." Mark licked his lips, trying to taste Jack on them.

"Right." Steve appeared to shake himself out of his dream. "I'll follow you. Drive slow."

"Yes, Officer." Mark saluted him.

Steve walked Mark to his car and waited for him to get in. After Mark started the engine, he sighed in exhaustion. In a vision, he imagined both Steve and Jack living with him. What were they going to do about Adam?

They finally came through the door after one in the morning. Mark was a walking zombie. Steve right behind him, Mark scuffed up the stairs, taking off his shirt, pausing in their bedroom. He looked at the photo of himself and Jack that still remained on the dresser. "I have to make a copy of that for him."

"Okay." Steve stood in front of him, helping him undress.

"Thank you, love."

"You just let me take care of you."

"I adore, adore, adore you." Mark sighed happily.

168

Once Mark was naked, Steve escorted him to the bathroom and loaded up Mark's toothbrush for him. "Here."

"You're a prince."

They scrubbed up side by side at the double basin. Steve helped Mark climb into bed. They snuggled together, Steve's hand on Mark's crotch, and Mark fell quickly to sleep.

Jack parked his Jag in the garage at the beach house and paused for a minute to gather his thoughts. He inhaled deeply, climbed out of the car and closed the garage door with a remote attached to his keys. Adam was standing at the front door when he arrived.

As Jack passed through it, he kissed Adam lightly on the lips.

"Is Mark okay?"

"Yes." Jack kicked off his shoes and tossed his keys down on the kitchen counter.

"What happened to him?" Adam leaned on the doorframe watching him.

Jack removed a bottle of whiskey and a glass from the cabinet. He poured some for himself, holding up the bottle to Adam. Adam declined. "He went on a photo shoot for a sunglasses company and the guys were really nasty." Jack shot down the booze and shivered at the burn. He wiped his lips with the back of his hand and set the glass on the counter, then met Adam's eyes. "He lucked out though. The LAPD SWAT team got a tip that the apartment was being used for drugs. They busted in and raided the place, finding Mark."

"Unbelievable."

"Mark said they showed up before anything actually happened. He got a slap in the jaw and was thrown around a little, but that's it." Jack capped the bottle and set it up in the cabinet. "Angel Loveday's partner, Billy Sharpe was the sergeant on the scene. Believe it?"

G.A. Hauser

Adam shook his head. "No."

"It's true." Jack walked across the room, intending on going up the stairs to bed. When he stood before Adam, he looked down at him curiously. "What?"

"What's going on between you and Mark?"

With a light tap of his finger on Adam's shoulder, Jack nudged Adam to go upstairs, following him, not answering until they were inside their bedroom. After Adam turned on the light and began disrobing, Jack sighed, "You know how much history Mark and I have."

Adam kept his back to Jack while they undressed.

While Jack removed his clothing, he wished he had a simple way of explaining this. "Adam."

Adam whipped his head around, glaring at him.

Jack closed the space between them and held Adam's shoulders tightly. "Please don't be upset."

After grinding his teeth in an obvious sign of fury, Adam replied, "Don't be upset? I meet you when that man had destroyed you, broke your heart, and now all of a sudden Mark wants you back and you're asking me not to be upset?"

"It's not like that. He doesn't want me back the way you're thinking."

"Sex. He wants to have sex with you. Isn't that the one thing you two haven't done yet?"

Jack flinched at the pain and venom coming from him. He reached out his hand and urged Adam to the bed to sit down. They were both naked, yet Jack knew Adam was feeling more vulnerable emotionally than physically. "I won't hurt you."

"Really? Haven't you already?"

Jack crushed Adam's hand in both of his. "Listen to me. I love you and I want to be brutally honest with you."

"It's more than Mark has been with you."

"What's that supposed to mean?" Jack asked.

170

"He's playing you for a fool."

"Stop." Jack released Adam's hand.

"Do you really think the 'fling' with Carl and Keith was all about the television show? Are you that naïve?"

A slight stabbing sensation made its way through Jack's chest. He stared at his hands as they relaxed on his lap. "Whatever. Look, what he and Steve do is their business."

"And what's our business? What do you want to do to Mark?"

Jack massaged his own temples as his exhaustion caught up to him. "You once told me about someone you propositioned." At the comment, Adam winced visibly. Jack shifted his posture on the bed, turning to look at him. Again he reached for Adam's hand. "You said you made a play for Jason, Ewan Gallagher's lover."

Adam's body tensed up and he tried to stand and get away. Jack held him firm.

"You knew Ewan Gallagher and Jason were in love. That they were in a committed relationship."

"What the hell's that got to do with anything?"

"It's a reminder that things sometimes get a little gray when it comes to attraction and commitment."

"What about Steve? Does he know you and Mark want to have sex?"

"Yes."

Adam blinked in confusion. "You said that so quickly I get the feeling you've all been discussing this behind my back."

"We have. A little. But it's not like it's been going on for weeks. This has all come up in the last few days."

"Why? Why has it come up?"

"A few reasons. One is that Mark met an old acquaintance of ours on a photo shoot. Janis Campbell, the photographer who used him for her book of male nudes back in ninety-three. She gave Mark a photo she had of Mark and I together."

"And? It lit the flame for him?"

"I think it brought back some memories. Painful ones."

Adam flopped back on the bed heavily, looking up at the ceiling. Jack reclined next to him, stroking Adam's flat belly gently. "I never lied about the way I feel about Mark."

"No." Adam laughed sarcastically. "You'll always be madly in love with him. I just wish you felt the same way about me."

"I do love you."

Adam met Jack's eyes. "Not with that passionate fire in your gut. I'm just comfortable. Convenient."

"Don't put words into my mouth."

"What do you want me to do?" Adam asked in frustration. "Spell it out for me, Larsen."

"Share him with me."

"I have no interest in Mark."

"What about Steve?"

"Steve?"

"Yes."

"Steve is in on this as well?"

"He is."

"Jesus. And I thought the Hollywood types were bad."

Jack grew impatient and sat up, wondering if he should sleep in the second bedroom.

With a hold on Jack's arm, Adam stayed him. "Are you asking me for permission?"

"I don't know what I'm asking anymore." Jack was so tired he just wanted to sleep.

"And if I say no? What then?"

"I need to go to sleep." Jack walked around to his side of the bed and pulled the sheet down, climbing in. Adam turned off the light and crawled in beside him.

In the darkness, hearing Adam's deep breathing, Jack curled around him and drew him close. In response, Adam intertwined his legs around Jack's and rested his head on Jack's chest. After giving Adam's forehead a kiss, Jack caressed Adam's long hair soothingly, comforting him. It was a lot to ask a man. Jack knew that. He didn't think he'd be willing to accept the bargain if the shoe were on the other foot. *Oh, Richfield, why is life around you so damn complicated?*

Chapter Fourteen

The sun blazed through the cracks in the blinds, Mark rolled over and burrowed into the pillows. It was Saturday and he had a right to sleep in. He didn't even peek at the clock. What did it matter? They could be lazy for once.

A warm hand alighted on his backside. Mark smiled happily. He assumed Steve was stirring awake as well, with the brightness in the room. Mark enjoyed the caresses and began squirming into the mattress and humming contentedly, savoring Steve's sensual touch. They had kicked off the sheets in the night, exposing themselves in the process. Steve's fingertips danced over each of Mark's ass cheeks and gently down the crack between to his thighs, back up to his lower back, sending tingles along Mark's spine.

A wet mouth sucked his shoulder. Mark felt Steve's tongue swirling around his skin tenderly. The head of Steve's cock poked his hip. Steve dipped his fingers through Mark's thighs, touching his balls from behind. Mark instantly opened his legs.

One finger stroked across his ring, teasing it, pressing into it lightly. Mark moaned, pushing his own hard cock into the mattress under him. The bed shifted.

Mark waited in anticipation. He felt Steve's bulk weighing the mattress down between his knees. A tantalizing tongue lapped at his bottom and Steve's hands parted his buttocks.

The quiet caressing had begun to get heated.

Steve ran his tongue from the base of his balls to his ass. Mark whimpered when the sensations intensified and opened his lips to gasp in delight, gripping the pillows tightly and shivering. Steve devoured him. Once his ring was wet from licks, Steve blew cool air on it. Mark moaned and humped the bed.

Very gently, Mark was urged to roll over onto his back. Mark flopped over like dead weight, his hair entangled over his face.

With a hand on each shin, Steve bent Mark's knees and urged his legs apart. Steve continued to lap where he had left off, giving Mark a complete tongue bath.

To be able to see, Mark pushed his hair off his face and propped himself up on the pillows and took a look at the action.

Steve had a grip on each of Mark's knees, leaning between them to lap at his balls and the skin of his inner thighs.

At the tongue tickling, Mark's cock was fully erect and throbbing with each slurp. Mark reached for it, squeezing it as it craved release, wiping the dewy stream of drops away from the tip with his thumb.

Steve sat up, staring at him. His hair was wild from his sleep, pointing in all directions, while his cock pointed in one— up. As Steve leaned close, he pressed the tip of his naked dick against Mark's ass, teasing it.

Unable to contain his excitement, Mark began stroking himself as he watched. Steve used his cock to explore Mark's genitals, rubbing it along Mark's sack and his thighs, leaving a trail of sticky pre-come.

Steve set his dick on target at Mark's ass and leaned forward, pressing it but not penetrating.

Mark quivered with a chill at the sensation of Steve's rounded cock head pushing against his back door. Mark quickened his hand motion with his rising passion, milking out more fluid.

Steve removed his dick from Mark's anus, shifting his weight so he was leaning over Mark's pelvis. When Mark felt Steve's cock rubbing against his knuckles, Mark opened his hand and enveloped Steve's dick with his own. With two hands Mark squeezed their lengths together, raising his hips in delight. He opened his eyes, not even realizing he had closed them, and found Steve's gaze riveted to their two shafts side by side.

Mark swiped at the glistening drops on Steve's slit, rubbing it on his own. Steve visibly shivered and his arm muscles tensed up as he propped himself up on the bed.

"Fuck!" Steve growled.

The first word of the new day.

"Let me get the lube," Steve said.

Mark released him at the sound of his urgency. As quickly as he could, Steve reached into the nightstand drawer and dug around for the tube. He smothered his dick in it and set back on his heels again, pushing Mark's legs apart to expose his ass.

"Oh, Richfield…" Steve moaned as he stared.

"I want you in."

A hiss of air blew out of Steve's lips in excitement. He drew closer, setting himself on target and leaned over Mark's body as he entered, slowly, but very deeply.

The sensation Mark adored, being filled, washed like a wave over his skin. When Steve had penetrated to the hilt, he paused, closing his eyes. Mark felt the throbbing of Steve's cock ripple through him and squeezed down on it.

Instantly, Steve began thrusting.

The view awed Mark. Steve's arms were engorged with blood, the veins protruding from the muscles holding him aloft. Mark caught glimpses through his own straddled legs of Steve's six-pack abs and tight legs. Steve humped him like a wild dog. Mark reached down to him, digging his fingers through Steve's unruly hair and massaging his scalp as it seemed the intensity began to overwhelm Steve.

"Shit! Shit!" Steve grunted, jamming his body against Mark's, pushing him higher on the bed with the power as he came. "Fuck!" Steve choked to gain air, hanging his head low. His hips finally stilled.

Like he needed time, taking a long moment, Steve didn't move. Mark loved it. He hated it when Steve pulled out. One last, deep, manly thrust in, and Steve disconnected their bodies.

A drop of sweat rolling down Steve's nose hit Mark's skin.

Once Steve's breathing softened, he grasped Mark's dick in both hands and lapped at the seeping tip.

Mark trembled down to his toes. Like a wildcat, Steve growled loudly and tried to fit all of Mark's cock into his mouth. Mark gasped at the sensation and raised body in response. With a tight gripping hold on the base, sucking to his knuckles and back, Steve drew hard on Mark's dick and quickened his rhythm.

"That's it...oh, love..." Mark began fucking Steve's mouth, holding onto the bed under them. Steve's tongue ran up and down in time with his mouth's strong suction. Mark felt his balls tighten up, and the rush to his loins blew him away. His lips opening to gasp in ecstasy, he cried loudly from the intensity.

The climax seemed to last forever. His skin lit on fire and he forced his eyes open to look at his lover. Steve was busy swallowing down his juice, milking him, slowing down his tempo. When Steve came up for air, Mark grabbed him by his shoulders and dragged him to his lips. Licking a drop of his own come from the corner of Steve's mouth, Mark moaned in delight and tasted his own sperm on Steve's tongue.

Once Steve was on top of Mark, he ground his re-hardened cock along Mark's, pressing him firmly against the bed with his weight.

Mark ate at his mouth, feeling Steve's unshaven morning jaw scratching his skin. Mark wrapped his legs around Steve's hips, locking his ankles behind him, and his arms around

Steve's back, never wanting to let him go.

As if Steve needed deep breaths of air, he parted from the kiss to pant, staring down at Mark's face, the sweat running down his skin. "I love you."

Mark lit up. "I love you too."

Steve dove down for more kisses. To deepen their kiss, Mark dug his hand into Steve's hair. Steve explored his mouth, wrapping his tongue around Mark's. Mark didn't want it to end. Steve pushed his cock down to contact Mark's balls. It was still slick with lubrication. Mark unlaced his ankles and used his thighs to clamp Steve's cock between them. Steve rocked his body to feel the friction.

"You're insatiable," Mark gasped.

"I can't get enough of you. Oh, Jesus. I want to be back in."

"Get in."

"No. No, babe. I'll let you rest." Steve flipped his cock back upright and dropped down on top of Mark heavily.

Mark felt the heaviness of Steve's body in pleasure and held him tight. In delight he felt Steve's breath on his neck as Steve recuperated. Mark caressed his back softly as they both settled down.

"That was intense."

"It always is with you," Mark whispered.

"No. That was really intense."

Mark smiled as Steve's hips pushed into his to emphasize his words.

"I was really worried last night, Mark."

"Shh. I'm okay."

"What are you going to do? Are you still going to model?"

When Steve leaned on his elbows to be able to see him, Mark wiped the sweat from Steve's brow. "I don't know what to do. I signed a bloody contract."

"I would think what happened last night would be the end of that contract. How could Arnold send you there? What the hell was he thinking?"

"I doubt very much he knew. The photographer, Randy, said he did freelance work. So perhaps Arnold had no clue."

"You have to call him and tell him."

"I intend to."

"Do you have any idea how frustrating it was not knowing where you were or how to find you?"

"Yes. I do. I'm sorry. I will give you all the details from now on." Mark pushed Steve's hair back from his forehead, feeling how overheated the lovemaking had gotten him.

"It's not that I'm treating you like you're weak. It's just common sense. If I were going out somewhere unknown, I'd want you to know."

"Yes. You're the sensible one of us. I should defer to your judgment."

Steve rolled to his side, his leg still overlapping Mark's, and propped himself up on a pillow. "I understand you hate being treated as weak. I do. I'm not doing that."

"I know." Mark touched Steve's wrist as Steve caressed his long hair.

"If anything happened to you, I'd die."

When Steve's eyes filled with water, Mark embraced him.

A sob broke from Steve's chest. "I couldn't live without you."

"Shh. Don't upset yourself." Mark squeezed him tight.

"When you die, I die."

"Hush! Don't be so morbid."

Steve pulled back so their gazes could meet again. Mark brushed at the flowing tears down Steve's cheeks. "I mean it." Steve inhaled a shaky breath. "I won't be on this planet without you."

The sentiment was so touching, Mark felt his body burn with love and devotion. "No one is going anywhere." He brushed back Steve's hair from his face. "Stop talking silly."

"Please don't let anything happen to you."

"Stop crying. Oh, Steven, you big mushball." Mark hugged him, rocking him. "Who says you're a tough cop? You're soft as pudding."

Steve cried as he laughed, burrowing under Mark's hair, cupping Mark's head to keep him close. "I never loved anyone like this. So deeply. So completely."

Mark melted at his words. "Do you say all the right things or what? I'm so hooked!" He kissed his neck.

Steve sat back again to see Mark's face. "Do you...do you love me more than you love Jack?"

First Mark stared into Steve's overflowing red eyes, then he kissed him, licking softly at his slack mouth. "I do. You are my partner. My number one man."

"Is that the truth?"

"It is. Cross my heart." Mark drew an X on his chest. "The minute I laid eyes on you at Parsons and Company, I was mad for you."

"Yeah?"

"Oh yes. You are the epitome of a man's man. Gorgeous, tough, smart, hilarious, fit...do I need to go on?"

"Did you feel that way about Jack when you met him in college?" Steve wiped at his eyes and nose.

Mark tried to think back to that moment. "No. Not as quickly as I fell for you. It was different then."

"Would you ever leave me for Jack?"

"No. Full stop. Never." Mark shook him.

"Promise?"

"Promise." Mark held up his hand in a vow. "Never. Never."

Steve wrapped his arms around him and squeezed him tight. "I love you so much."

Mark hugged him, feeling his boiling heat against his skin. "Don't you ever worry. You hear me? That is one thing you never have to concern yourself about. I am yours 'til death, my love."

"Thank you…oh, baby, thank you."

"Don't thank me, love. I'm the lucky one."

Jack rolled over on the bed, reaching out his arm. He felt a void instead of a body. He sat up and looked around the room. No Adam. He tossed off the covers and hunted him down. Adam was sipping coffee with the morning paper on the patio.

Once he pushed the sliding door back, Jack stepped outside naked. He took the cup from Adam's hand, set it on the ground, then picked Adam up and carried him into the house.

"What now, Sampson?" Adam sighed, the newspaper falling to the floor.

"You left the bed a bit early." Jack carried him up the stairs.

"I didn't want to wake you."

"Since when?" Jack lowered him to the mattress and unzipped Adam's shorts, yanking them down his legs with his briefs. He tossed the clothing on the floor and settled between Adam's legs.

"Jack…"

Though it was said like a scold, Jack ignored him and dipped the tip of Adam's cock into his mouth. "You showered without me too?" He sniffed around Adam's balls, smelling the familiar aroma of their soap.

"Like I said…"

"Shut up. Stop acting like there's a problem between us." Jack worked on Adam's cock but it didn't seem to be

181

responding to his attention.

"Acting?"

Jack ignored him and enveloped his soft cock completely, closing his eyes and drawing on it until he felt it begin to harden.

"Christ, Larsen, what are you doing to me?"

"Giving you a blowjob," Jack mumbled quickly and continued.

"More like a mind blow."

"Shut up and come." Jack felt Adam's legs tense and his dick become fully erect. "Better." He sucked deep, completely sinking all of Adam's cock into his mouth.

"Just don't fantasize it's Mark's cock you're sucking."

Jack gaped at him, allowing Adam's prick to fall from his lips. "What the fuck did you say?"

"You heard me."

Jack sat up and glared at him. "You're determined to make this an issue."

"Isn't it one already?" Adam's cock quickly softened.

"Why does it have to be?"

"You tell me that."

"Fine. You know what? Forget it." Jack stood off the bed and headed to the shower. Why was Steve able to understand this and not Adam? "Christ, what's the big fucking deal?"

Standing under the water, Jack soaped himself, his temper rising quickly from his frustration. "I'll do it with or without your blessing, buddy. Your choice."

They had dozed again. Mark slowly came to the conscious world and opened his eyes. The clock read ten after ten. He yawned. Steve shifted on top of him heavily. Mark ran his hands over Steve's hair and neck, rousing him gently.

"I don't want to get up," Steve moaned.

"You don't have to." Mark smiled, circling his fingers down Steve's bronze shoulders.

"We should run before it gets too hot."

"Can't we take a day off?"

"We did yesterday and the day before, and the day before, because of your stupid sessions."

"Groan..." Mark complained.

"We need to do a long one."

"Groan!" Mark echoed louder.

"Come on, Mr. Richfield. Don't make me spank you."

"Slave driver."

Steve leaned up on his arms and kissed Mark's lips, then climbed off him to wash up in the bathroom.

Mark stretched like a cat, wriggling with a chill down his spine, and stood, his arms reaching over his head. He caught sight of the photo of him and Jack and smiled at it. "Right. I'm here. I'm here." Mark scuffed to the bathroom to brush his teeth and hair. "How far do we have to run, Mr. Slave Driver?"

"Ten." Steve spat out the toothpaste and rinsed his mouth.

Mark let out a long low sound of disapproval.

"Tough." Steve squeezed Mark's ass in his hand. "Gotta keep the meat firm."

"Yes, sir!" Mark jumped.

"Good soldier." Steve kissed Mark's jaw and left the bathroom.

Mark smiled at his reflection in the mirror. He was the luckiest fucker around.

"Are you going to give me the silent treatment all day?" Jack asked, pouring himself a cup of coffee as Adam sat at the kitchen island counter and continued to read the paper.

"Maybe."

"Why?"

Adam raised his eyebrow at Jack in disbelief.

Jack pulled a stool closer to him, sat down and leaned his elbow on the counter, holding his coffee mug. "Is it because you're jealous of Mark?"

"Yes! Duh! You sure you have a degree in law?" Adam shook his head in annoyance.

"But I'm not leaving you for him."

"Not yet anyway." Adam flipped the pages of the newspaper.

"No. I have no intention of doing that. Adam, we have a good relationship."

Another sarcastic chortle erupted from Adam. "Oh, yeah. Sure we do."

Jack tore the paper away from Adam and shoved it on the floor "Look at me when we have a discussion."

"What the fuck are you, my father?" Adam's brown eyes blazed.

"Are you determined to end this?" Jack waved his hand to gesture at their living arrangements.

"I'm not the one who's chomping at the bit to fuck another man."

"With you. Not behind your back, not without you. With you."

"I don't want to screw Richfield. Or Steve. Do you get it?"

"So if I do, we're finished?"

"Now you finally got it. Took you long enough." Adam walked around the counter to pick up his paper.

"Don't make it a choice."

"But it is. It's a choice."

Jack covered his eyes with his hand tiredly. "Do you know

how long I've waited for Mark to say yes?"

"Ask me if I care." Adam leaned on the counter across from him, reading his paper.

"Ever since we played ball in college. Almost twenty years, Adam."

"You will not convince me that it's right, Larsen. Save your breath."

"Why can Steve understand? Huh? How come Steve can comprehend what this is all about and you can't? Are you telling me you're not as smart as a blue-collar cop?"

"Smart? You call Steve smart for allowing Mark his deluded sexual fantasies? I'm beginning to think I don't know you at all anymore."

Jack rubbed his rough jaw; his head began to hurt. "Right. So if I go with Mark, I have to move out."

"Bingo." Adam didn't make eye contact.

"We're supposed to go out for Chinese food with them tonight."

"And?"

"I want us to go."

"Sure, Jack. Whatever." Adam set his mug in the sink and left the room.

After he left, Jack stared out the back sliding door at the ocean. He released a heavy sigh, then passed through the doorway and stood with his coffee cup, staring out at the cresting waves, feeling the cool breeze on his skin. Was it worth it? Was having Mark worth sacrificing Adam?

The last mile was brutal. Mark felt like his ears were ringing. Every time he planted his foot in front of him, he could hear his blood pressure like a loud echo. Ten miles in near ninety-degree heat, at a fast pace, was killing him. He was thirty-seven, not twenty. His knees ached, his feet burned, he was dehydrated and dripping with sweat.

"Almost there, Mark. Almost there."

Finally hearing Steve gasp, Mark realized the run was as hard for him. They rounded the corner of their street. Steve accelerated his speed to a sprint. Even though Mark knew it was coming, he still dreaded it. His legs feeling numb, pumping, pounding the pavement, Mark clenched his fists and forced his body to respond.

They flew the last few meters, brushing soaked arms and shoulders as they did. Steve whacked the door with his palm and dropped down to the grass. Mark doubled over, laboring for air. "The key. The bleedin' key." Mark reached out.

Steve pulled off his running shoe and threw it at him, still struggling to breathe.

It hit him and bounced off the front pathway. Mark reached for it, feeling dizzy. He untied the lace, pulled the key off the string and dropped the shoe. He staggered inside and stuck his head under the running cold water in the kitchen sink.

Mark turned off the tap and dripped into the basin. He could hear Steve behind him. Mark pushed the hair out of his eyes and peered back as Steve offered him a bottle of water.

Leaning back against the sink, Mark caught his breath as he sucked down the water.

"Good job, Mark. Good run."

"I can't wait for fall." Mark inhaled, choking on a sip of water that went down the wrong pipe.

Steve approached him and licked the dripping water off Mark's cheek. "Mm, salty."

Mark laughed with an effort.

"Want ice on your dick?"

"Yes. That was lovely."

Steve set his water bottle on the table and opened the freezer, taking out the tray. With a click of the plastic mold, he popped an ice cube into his hand. He drew back the waistband of Mark's running shorts and jock strap.

When the ice hit Mark's boiling crotch, he jumped first, then relaxed. Steve massaged the melting cube all over his dick and balls.

It turned to water in seconds. Steve reached for another one and dropped it down Mark's pants, taking two more to hold, running them over Mark's nipples and chest.

Mark shivered in pleasure, closing his eyes.

"Christ, this is so erotic," Steve crooned, licking Mark's icy, erect nipples.

"We're getting the floor all wet again."

"I'll mop it up later." Steve smoothed his melting piece of ice down Mark's chest to his belly button, sliding his hand into his wet clothes.

Goose pimples covered Mark's skin as Steve's cold, wet hand kneaded his anatomy.

"Look at you." Steve let go a breath through his teeth.

At the comment, Mark opened his eyes, and glanced down. Steve had his organ exposed from the jock strap and his shorts yanked down his thighs. "You always turn me obscene."

"It's so easy to do with a body like yours." Steve drove his hand under Mark's wet testicles, massaging them deeply.

A shiver of passion washed over Mark's length. He clenched his fingers around the counter behind him and rose onto the balls of his feet.

Steve began stroking Mark's shaft at the same time as he fondled between Mark's legs. The chills kept coursing over Mark's body, turning into a desperate yearning to come.

"You gorgeous motherfucker." Steve leaned down and licked the tip of Mark's cock. "Your come tastes so fucking good."

Mark opened his lips to gasp with the next wave of delight.

When he looked down, seeing Steve's tongue dipping into his slit, his dick fully engorged to a blushing red as the teasing drove him insane. Steve suddenly released the contact. "Where are you going?" Mark scolded.

"Hold on. Hang on." Steve raced around the room to a drawer.

When he produced a tape measure, Mark choked in disbelief. "Steven! How juvenile."

"Where do you measure from?"

"Steve!" Mark's cheeks grew hot from his embarrassment.

"Holy shit!"

"Steven, get up." Mark tugged on his arm.

"Oh, no way."

"Steve. This is horrible."

"Ten!" Steve held up the tape. "Ten fucking inches!"

"You have to be mistaken." Mark waved the tape away. "Behave."

Steve tossed the tape measure on the counter, got to his knees and sucked like mad.

When Mark could gather his thoughts, he looked down and found Steve's cock out of his shorts. He was masturbating at the same time as he was giving Mark head. Just the sight was enough to send Mark reeling. He arched his back and gripped onto the sink for dear life. Steve went wild below him, grunting and groaning like a sex fiend.

"Ah! Ah! Ah!" Mark cried, pumping his load into Steve's eager mouth while Steve's come pelted his shin. "Oh, Christ, oh, bloody Christ..." His knees gave out and his arms held him up as he was drained. Still gasping, swallowing down a dry throat, he pried open his eyes and glanced down.

Steve was beaming at him. "You magnificent fucker."

Mark laughed in exhaustion. "You'll kill me. You will."

Slowly climbing up Mark's body, Steve pressed him back

against the counter and kissed him. Mark tasted the familiar essence of his come. He had kissed Steve after so many blowjobs, he knew both their flavors by heart.

Finally sated, Steve rested his forehead on Mark's shoulder, lightly toying with Mark's limp dick. "You are so amazing."

"Me?" Mark leaned heavily on Steve as he recovered.

"You, you, you," Steve sung tiredly.

"Come. Let's shower. We have to figure out which Chinese restaurant to go to tonight and make reservations."

With a low moan, Steve stood back from Mark, allowing him to move. Stiff and tired, Mark climbed the stairs with Steve holding onto his hips for the ride up. Mark dragged them both into the bathroom and finished stripping. "I need a damn nap."

"Oh, God, yeah." Steve yawned, reaching in to turn on the water. "Shower, call the restaurant, nap."

Jack finished his workout in their home gym and showered. Adam was still sulking somewhere on the beach outside. When the phone rang, Jack checked the time. It was nearing three. "Hello?"

"Hi, Jackie."

"Hi, Mark." Jack's skin prickled at his voice.

"How does Yujean Kang's sound? Around seven-ish?"

"Fine. How are you feeling?"

"Good. Very good, love."

"I'm glad. I was very worried about you." Jack heard Adam coming in through the back sliding door. Jack walked with the phone to meet up with him.

"I really am fine, love. So? You want us to pick you up? We don't mind."

Jack cupped the phone. "Do you want them to pick us up on their way?"

"It doesn't matter."

At the curt reply, Jack tried not to be annoyed. He said to Mark, "Yes. That's fine. So? Around seven?"

"Yes, Jackie."

"Okay. See you then."

"Bye, baby."

Jack pushed the disconnect button on the telephone and placed it down on the counter.

Adam wore only a pair of khaki shorts and his sunglasses were resting on the top of his head. As if he were ignoring Jack, he washed his hands at the kitchen sink and picked up an apple from a fruit bowl.

While he crunched it and chewed, Jack approached him and dug his hands through Adam's long brown mane, removing his sunglasses and tossing them on the counter. His hair was nearly as long as Mark's now and he looked delicious.

"Bite?"

Jack bit into the offered apple. "Thanks." With small steps, Jack walked Adam backwards so he was leaning against the counter, then Jack pushed their crotches together. As Adam ate, Jack kept toying with his hair, pulling it back into a ponytail behind his head.

"It's long."

"It is." Jack smiled. "I love it."

"I haven't had it this long since high school." Adam took another bite of the apple, offering it to Jack again.

"I'm okay." Jack declined the offer, his cock growing hard at the sight of Adam's handsome face and the feel of his body. "You're damn sexy, you know that?"

"You kissing up?"

"No. I'm telling you what I think." Jack pushed his cock harder into Adam.

"What do you intend to do with that thing in your pants?"

Adam tossed the apple core into the sink behind him.

"What do you want me to do with it?" Jack nibbled Adam's jaw.

As if finally giving in, Adam wrapped himself around Jack and held him, exhaling a deep sigh. "I don't want to lose you."

"I'm not going anywhere." Jack squeezed him tight.

"Oh, he-man, what am I going to do with you?"

"Sex before dinner would be nice." Jack chewed on his neck.

Adam leaned back to see Jack's face, then pecked his lips. "Let's go."

Jack picked Adam up, tossing him over his shoulder, taking advantage of his vulnerable position and rubbing his hands all over Adam's bottom and balls.

"You're lucky you're so damn adorable, he-man."

"I am lucky. And I'm about to get luckier." Jack slipped his finger inside the leg of Adam's shorts and squirmed in.

"Ah! You're so wicked. Tormenting a helpless man."

"I haven't even started yet." Jack laughed, carrying him up the stairs.

"I can't wait."

Jack was very glad his loving Adam was back.

Chapter Fifteen

Steve parked in the driveway of Adam's Malibu home. "Should we both go in?"

"Yes. In case they're not ready." Mark opened the car door.

Steve obviously agreed, shutting off the engine and following Mark. Just as Mark was about to ring the bell, Jack opened the door.

"Hello. We weren't sure if you were ready."

"We are." Jack smiled sweetly at him. "Hello, Steve."

"Mr. Larsen." Steve grinned wickedly at him.

Adam stepped out. "Hello, men. Mark, how are you after your ordeal?"

"Good, Adam. Thanks for asking."

Adam walked Mark to the car. "Did you call Arnold about it?"

"I did, but he's not answering any of his lines on the weekend. I've left several messages." Mark opened the back door for him.

"He really needs to know."

"Yes. I shall try him first thing Monday."

Mark sensed Jack close behind him. He glanced over his shoulder to see Jack's smile.

"Look at you in your summer whites." Jack ran his hand over Mark's bottom. "No underwear lines. My, oh my."

"Steve did the same thing. I'll have a big wet stain soon if you both continue to tease me." Mark nudged Jack. "You sit up front with Steven. Let me keep Adam company." Mark joined Adam in the backseat. "So, what happens now, Adam? After I let Arnold know?"

"Well, they'll most likely contact the Better Business Bureau, along with several other watchdog agencies and blacklist them."

"Good."

"What client was it?" Adam asked, folding his hands over his black slacks.

"Sunspec? A sunglasses company. I've never heard of them before."

"Arnold should call Sunspec and let them know as well, so they don't farm out any more work to those idiots." Adam addressed Steve, "Hey, copper, how long before Mark knows what's going to happen to those guys?"

"Don't know. Mark could call Sgt. Billy to find out."

"Sgt. Billy?" Adam cocked his head curiously.

"Didn't Jack tell you?" Mark leaned against Adam's shoulder. "The officer who saved me was Angel Loveday's partner, Billy Sharpe."

"Yes. That's right," Adam said. "What a weird coincidence."

"Yes. It was." Mark ran his hand through Adam's hair.

Adam jerked his head around to stare at him.

"It's so long." Mark played with it.

Adam shivered visibly and nudged Mark's hand away. "Behave yourself. How many cocks do you need exactly?"

Steve choked and Jack rubbed his eyes.

"Is that an offer, handsome?" Mark stroked his hand up

Adam's leg.

"Good grief," Adam sighed. "You are walking sex, Mr. Richfield."

"So I've been told." Mark leaned his head on Adam's shoulder, relaxing on him, his legs falling to a wide straddle.

"And I hear you want to play doctor with my man."

"Yes. Guilty as charged." Mark nestled against Adam. "Damn, you smell nice."

"Ditto. I don't know if it's your cologne or your pheromones." Adam inhaled deeply.

Mark noticed Steve and Jack exchange quick glances.

"So..." Adam continued, "Steve's game, Jack's game, you're game..."

Mark moved in the seat to face him, running his hand up Adam's thigh, stopping just before he contacted his crotch. As he nuzzled Adam's hair, Mark licked his sideburn with the tip of his tongue.

"Oh, Jesus," Adam moaned.

Jack twisted around in the seat to see what was going on. At Adam's blushing cheeks, he smiled in delight. "Having fun, Adam?"

"Did you plan this, Larsen?" Adam asked.

"Nope. Did I plan anything, Mark?"

"Plan what?" Mark tickled Adam's earlobe with his tongue. "You taste good," he purred. "I love the way you look with your hair long." He dug his hand into it again.

"Holy fuck." Adam shifted in his seat.

Steve broke up laughing. Soon after, Jack joined him.

"What's so funny?" Mark asked. "Share with the backseat, please." He gazed at Adam's lap. "Ohh, nice hard-on, love."

Steve roared, wiping his eyes as he choked up with hilarity.

"Jack!" Adam exclaimed.

"I did not plan this." Jack held up his hands.

"Oh, what the fuck," Adam moaned. "Mark, get over here."

"Yes?"

Adam grabbed Mark's jaw and kissed him. At the shock, Mark's eyes sprang open.

"Oh, God." Steve cracked up. "I can't drive. I have to pull over to see this."

Tingles washed over Mark's skin. "Mm, Adam. Nice. You didn't tell me he was a good kisser, Jackie." He drew Adam closer, experimenting with his tongue as Adam's hand pressed against his body. Mark opened his eyes and sat back to see what Adam had in mind.

"Jack." Adam rubbed his palm down the inseam of Mark's white pants where he had grown hard. "Sweet Mother of God!"

Steve stopped for a traffic signal and twisted to look back at them. "Oh, I measured it. Ten fucking inches."

"Steven," Mark chided. "That's personal. And juvenile."

Jack couldn't stop laughing. "This is too funny."

Adam dropped his head on the seat back. "All right. You're all crazy, but I'm in."

"In?" Mark blinked. "In what?"

"In you, Richfield," Jack clarified. "He wants a piece of you."

"Really? Good." Mark stared at Adam's profile. "You are damn good looking, Adam Lewis."

After a soft moan, Adam slid his hand around Mark's leg and ran his palm down Mark's length again.

"A wet spot. I knew it." Mark clicked his tongue. "Serves me right for wearing white."

"Oh, Jack," Adam whimpered. "He is amazing."

"I know, Adam." Jack breathed deeply. "I know."

"How am I supposed to eat?" Steve whined. "I'm so fucking hot I could spurt. Give me a play-by-play, Larsen. What are they doing?"

Jack twisted around to look. "Mark's sacked out on Adam's shoulder and Adam is running his right hand along Mark's hard dick."

"Ohhh," Steve moaned.

"He's so easy to please," Mark whispered to Adam.

"I imagine a steady diet of you has him very pleased." Adam gently leaned his head against Mark's.

"I'm so glad we're all in love. Isn't this amazing, Jackie?"

"It is, Mark. Absolutely amazing."

"You love me?" Adam asked in surprise.

"Yes. I adore you. You've made Jack so happy." Mark ran his fingertips along Adam's leg playfully.

"Really?" Adam met Mark's eyes.

"Yes. Really. Why does love have to be confined to one? Where is that written? Is it some Bible scripture? Why can't I love you all?"

"You can, Mark." Steve pulled into the restaurant lot.

"Thank you, Steven." Mark smiled proudly.

"Come here." Adam cupped Mark's face.

Mark tilted to look and Adam kissed him generously. "You are sweeter than sugar."

"Thank you, Adam. That's high praise from someone I respect as much as you."

Steve found a parking spot and twisted around to the backseat. "You need a minute, Mark?"

Mark looked down at his crotch and sighed. "It's my own flamin' fault."

"Don't worry. We'll hide you." Adam nudged him.

Jack climbed out and opened the back door for Mark. Mark

196

stepped out and all three men stood back to have a look at him.

"Well?" Mark asked.

"Do you always go commando?" Adam asked.

"No. Not always. Steven? Am I obscene?"

"No. You're okay. No one will notice." Mark caught Steve winking at Jack.

They walked as a group to the front entrance. As Adam and Steve spoke with the hostess, Jack kissed Mark's cheek. "You are wonderful."

"Thank you, Jackie. Why am I wonderful?"

"For including Adam the way you did."

"Why shouldn't he be included? He's your man." When Adam spun back around to them, Mark threw him a kiss, making him blush. "He's darling with his long hair."

"He is. I know." Jack directed Mark behind the other two to their table.

Once they were comfortable with menus in their hands, Mark perused the selection hungrily. "We should order four dishes and share."

"Definitely." Steve licked his lips.

"How about the crispy beef?" Jack suggested.

"Why don't we get one of each?" Adam offered.

"Yes. Let Adam order for us." Mark set his menu down. "Adam, can you do the honors?"

"I would be happy to." Adam smiled in delight.

Jack shot Mark a satisfied smile, leaned on Adam's shoulder and looked at what he had chosen for their meal.

"I love you," Steve whispered to Mark adoringly.

"You're being such a good sport." Mark held his hand under the table.

"Your gain is my gain, lover."

"True." Mark knew Steve wanted a kiss. Instead Mark

197

squeezed his hand tightly in the crowded room.

After they were served drinks, Adam went to work ordering their food. Once he had finished, they handed off their menus to the waitress.

"I can't wait. I'm starved." Steve toyed with his chopsticks.

"Did you guys do anything today?" Adam asked, sipping his cocktail.

"We ran." Steve drummed the sticks on the table until Mark stopped him.

"Ten bloody miles," Mark moaned, rolling his eyes.

"In this heat?" Adam asked. "Are you nuts?"

"Yes!" Mark replied.

"Just get a treadmill, like ours." Jack drank his beer.

"Treadmills are for sissies," Steve claimed.

"Hey," Adam said. "Who you calling a sissy?"

"I don't mind it normally." Mark leaned his elbows on the table. "But it's brutal once the temperature gets over eighty."

"It's been well over ninety this past week," Jack said. "No way should you be running in it."

Mark gestured to Steve in frustration. "Tell him that."

"You can get heatstroke, Steve," Adam said.

"I do. I swear. I have to stick my head under the cold water the moment we get home." Mark stirred his drink with a plastic swizzle stick, sucked it dry and set it on the table.

"I put ice on his cock." Steve grinned wickedly.

"Oh!" Adam shivered. "Torture."

"He likes it."

Mark blushed. "Do you have to tell them all our secrets?"

"We're about to have an orgy." Steve laughed. "Don't tell them I put an ice cube on your hot dick?"

Adam wriggled in his seat. "Christ, how am I going to last through dinner?"

"It's a good thing we're all eating that garlic eggplant." Mark looked around the area quickly. "Because we'll all be kissing each other."

"Okay." Adam raised his hands in surrender. "I give up. Just let me ravish him now."

"You're so cute," Mark giggled at Adam.

"Thank you, Adam," Jack whispered, but they all could hear.

"You don't blame me for being cautious. I mean, look at him, Jack."

"Are they talking about me?" Mark asked Steve.

"Yes, cutie. But don't worry." Steve snuck a kiss to his cheek.

"I know. Why do you think I've been madly in love with him all my adult life?"

"Oh, Jackie…" Mark reached for him across the table.

"It's okay, Mark." Jack squeezed his hand quickly.

"It's the fucking combination of his looks and his innocence. It's so goddamn sexy." Adam finished his drink down to the ice.

"Wow." Mark lit up. "What a sweet thing to say."

"I assume he's a bottom."

"Yes," Jack confirmed.

"Damn." Adam squirmed in his chair.

"Crispy beef? Cashew chicken?" the waitress announced. "Prawn with glazed walnut? Garlic eggplant?" She set their dishes down on the table.

"Mm, that smells wonderful," Mark said.

"Adam, you did good." Steve dove in.

"You're so classy, Adam." Mark scooped out some rice.

"Thank you, guys." Adam smiled modestly.

"And you shall be amply rewarded," Mark added.

G.A. Hauser

"Can't fucking wait," Adam growled.

"Taste." Steve held up a morsel to Mark's lips in his chopsticks.

Mark ate it, moaning, "Mmm." When he did, he noticed Jack and Adam exchange winks.

Completely buzzed on sweet cocktails, Mark was glad Steve was driving because he was well over the limit himself.

"Are we coming in?" Steve asked as he pulled into Adam's driveway.

"Are you kidding?" Adam laughed at the joke. "I hope you brought your jammies."

Jack was smiling wickedly as he followed Adam to the front door.

"You all right, cutie?" Steve cuddled his arms around Mark.

"I'm wonderful."

"I'll say." Steve chewed Mark's jaw.

Once they were inside Adam and Jack's beautiful beachfront home, Adam asked, "Can I get anyone anything?"

"Oh, yes." Mark sauntered over to him.

"Come here, you sex god." Adam opened his arms.

"Here we go," Steve said. "Where do I start?"

"Why don't we do this upstairs?" Jack grabbed Steve's hand and Steve clasped Mark's.

As Mark climbed the stairs behind Steve, Adam was connected to Mark's butt, nipping it.

Jack began undressing. Steve watched Jack as he took off his own clothing. Mark gaped in awe at the male flesh being exposed. Adam quickly stripped down to nothing.

Suddenly, all three men were naked, looking at him.

"Hullo…" Mark laughed.

"Why are you still dressed?" Adam moved to stand behind him.

Steve lowered to his knees and chewed Mark's erection through his white slacks.

"Ah!" Mark gasped.

Jack dug his hand through Mark's hair and brought him to his lips. At the touch of Jack's mouth, Mark's knees grew weak.

Steve opened Mark's trousers and dragged them down his thighs.

Adam dropped to his knees and licked Mark's bottom, nibbling his cheeks.

The excitement in Mark was unmatched. His heart was pounding under his ribs. In need of a deep inhale of breath, he broke from Jack's kiss and groaned loudly, gripped Jack's shoulders to keep from falling.

"Give me that tongue," Jack insisted.

Steve sucked his cock, teasing it, not satisfying it. Behind him, Adam was making hickeys on his ass cheeks, spreading them apart and lapping at his ring.

At the thrill, Mark reached to Jack's lips, trying to concentrate on their kiss while so much stimulation was making him wild. The tricks and trills Jack performed in his mouth were making him so hot he was about to come. This was his Jack Charles Larsen, his rock, his savior during all his college years and beyond.

"Take me," Mark begged him. "Take me first."

Adam broke contact and hurried to the nightstand. He tossed more than enough condoms and lubrication onto the bed.

"Come here, gorgeous." Jack slowly walked Mark to the king-sized mattress.

"Jack. My Jackie…" Mark choked up. "I've waited a lifetime for this."

"I know. Me too."

As Jack prepared himself, Adam took over where Jack had left off, kissing Mark, digging through his hair. Mark reciprocated, loving Adam's long silky locks. When Mark opened his eyes, Steve was standing beside them, pumping his own cock slowly as he observed.

"Baby?" Mark asked him.

"You enjoy it, Mark. You guys have waited long enough."

Adam and Steve stood together and played with each other's cocks while watching Jack and Mark.

"You ready, my love?"

"Yes, Jackie. I've been ready for nearly twenty years."

"Lie on your back. I want to see your face."

Mark obeyed, tears threatening.

"Look at you," Jack sighed.

"Oh, Jackie-blue..." Mark dabbed at his eyes.

Jack knelt between his legs, pushing Mark's knees back towards his chest.

On first contact, Mark closed his eyes and had to force them to open to look at his beautiful best friend. Jack's cock was inside him. Mark was about to combust at the thrill.

"I won't last, lover."

"I know, Jackie."

"Yes," Jack moaned. How long had he waited? How many times had he imagined this?

He tried to hold back. He wanted it to last. It had to last. He had to slow down.

He gazed at Mark's body under him, Mark's enormous, engorged cock bobbing with each thrust, his face stained with emotional tears of joy. Jack couldn't believe it was actually happening and it wasn't just one of his many dreams.

While Mark took Jack's cock up his back passage, he noticed Adam move closer. Adam kept touching Jack's body as Jack thrust his hips into Mark. Steve lay next to Mark, watching eagerly.

"Oh, my fucking God..." Jack shivered, jamming his body into Mark's.

"That's it baby...that's it," Mark cried as Steve kissed his tears.

A deep, masculine grunt filled the air as Jack climaxed.

Mark felt his skin burst with chills. "That's it, yes, my baby." His tears ran down his cheeks.

Slowly Jack recovered, opening his eyes and staring down at Mark. "It was so fucking worth the wait."

Mark smiled, then started laughing with his relief at finally having Jack's physical love. "I adore you."

When he began pulling out, Jack shook his body as if to come back to life. "Wow."

"Adam?" Mark reached out.

"Yes."

"Bring it here." Mark pointed to his lips. He sat up, making room for Adam to lie back on the bed.

When Adam made himself comfortable, Mark nestled between his legs and began licking his balls.

"Oh my...oh my, oh my," Adam exclaimed.

The minute Jack returned from washing up, he leaned across the bed and kissed Adam's lips while Steve licked at Adam's nipples and chest.

Mark sucked Adam deep and hard. Moaning in pleasure at serving such a wonderful, generous man, Mark savored Adam's scent and taste. He opened his eyes to see Steve smiling at him wickedly. Mark smiled back and resumed his task.

A ripple of pleasure from Adam's organ passed Mark's lips. He increased his speed and depth. Adam inhaled deeply as he climaxed. Adam's hips rose and began fucking Mark's mouth quickly. The moment Mark dipped his finger into Adam's ass, he tasted Adam's load instantly. He swallowed him down, groaning in pleasure, getting every drop.

The minute Mark sat back to catch his breath, both Steve and Jack went for his kiss. Mark laughed in delight and grabbed Steve's face, planting one on him, wondering if he was curious about the taste of Adam's come.

Steve broke from Mark's kiss. "I have to fuck someone."

"Take your pick." Jack gestured to himself or Adam.

"Holy crap." Steve pumped his cock at the decision.

In response, Jack moved to his hands and knees. Steve stumbled off the bed to get a condom.

"Come here, sweet stuff." Adam craned his finger at Mark.

"I want to watch." Mark pointed to Jack.

"Me too. Come here and watch with me."

Steve knelt behind Jack, wasting no time. "I'm in, Larsen."

"I know, Miller." Jack laughed.

Mark inched under Jack to get at his cock while Adam kissed Jack's lips. As Steve humped Jack's ass, Mark closed his mouth around Jack's length. It was sublime. The scent of soap and his delicious musk mixed in Mark's nose. How many years had he denied himself this treat? He must have been mad, completely insane.

Jack hardened to stone in his mouth. Mark tried to keep up with Steve's thrusting hips. *I need to taste you. Please.*

Jack was overwhelmed. Now his cock was in Mark's mouth. How many days back in college did he want to beg Mark to do it? Forever. Forever and a day.

Steve came, jamming his hips into Jack tightly. Jack waited as patiently as he could, but all he could think about was Mark's mouth.

The second Steve pulled out, Jack knelt up on the bed, bringing Mark with him. Mark crouched in front of him, sucking.

Not quite believing what he was seeing, Jack wanted to pinch himself to convince himself it was real and not yet another Mark Antonious fantasy. "Mark."

Mark looked up, his cock in his mouth.

"Let me lie down. Savor it."

Mark released his contact and waited. Steve had gone to wash up and Adam reclined on the bed, watching him and Mark together again.

Jack repositioned himself to relax, his head propped up for better viewing. He nodded his readiness. Mark moved to lie between his quads, going back to his task of sucking his dick.

Jack watched Mark in action. His beloved pretty boy giving him head was beyond words.

Adam leaned on Jack's shoulder. "Enjoying it?"

"Hell, yeah."

"He looks as though he is as well."

"He is." Steve sat down on Jack's other side. "He loves sucking cock. Taking it up the ass. Everything."

Adam snuggled closer to Jack, smoothing his hand over Jack's broad chest as he watched.

Jack wanted to close his eyes at the intensity, but he just couldn't bear the thought of not seeing Mark doing this. *Jesus. Finally! Mark is giving me a frickin' blowjob. Hallelujah!*

Mark was doing his best. This one meant something special. It was his Jack. His best friend, his confidant, his ally.

Not wanting Jack to come too quickly, Mark left his cock for a moment to lap at his balls. He tasted divine.

Jack's soft, curling blond pubic hair contrasted with the three dark bushes around him. Mark rubbed his face into it, moving again to his shaft, devouring it. He was dying to taste Jack's come. Almost two decades of waiting. The wait was over.

Mark got to his knees for better access. He gripped the base of Jack's cock and went for it.

Jack's body shivered. This second climax was going to outdo the first, he had no doubt. Adam nibbled his nipple, Steve caressed his hair, and Mark, Mark was eating his cock greedily. A wave washed over Jack. He tensed his muscles. Mark felt it, going crazy on him. A finger found his ass. The minute Mark pushed in, Jack arched his back and came, shuddering at the intensity, telling himself, *"This is Mark."*

At the first pulsating throb, Mark felt Jack's come enter his mouth. It was bliss. Mark moaned in ecstasy, sucking harder, pumping his mouth faster. Another burst of Jack's come coated his tongue. Mark savored it, rolling it in his mouth before he swallowed it, then he milked Jack's cock for every last delightful drop. When he could, Mark looked up at his ex-roommate's blue eyes. The love he found there made his skin tingle.

"Baby," Mark whimpered.

Jack, seemingly speechless, reached out for him.

The desire to hold him great, Mark crawled up Jack's body, and connected to his mouth. Adam licked at that connection on one side, while Steve did on the other.

Finally resting on Jack's enormous muscular length was a triumph for Mark. It had been very long overdue.

When Mark sat back to smile at Jack's weary expression, he asked, "How did I do, Jackie? As good as your fantasies?"

"God, yes."

"Your turn, Mark?" Adam asked softly.

Mark wriggled on Jack excitedly, flopped to his back next to Jack and announced, "Take me! I'm yours!"

Jack moved to lie on his side and kissed Mark. Steve hurried to Mark's cock and plunged it into his mouth while Adam nestled between Mark's legs and sucked on his balls.

A rush of desire cascaded over Mark's body. Three of the men he loved most in the world were here. Sharing, giving him pleasure. It just didn't get any better than that.

His skin tingling as Steve and Adam worked in tandem, Mark parted from Jack's mouth for deep breaths. Jack watched first his face and then the action down below. Adam rolled Mark's balls over his tongue, and pushed his finger inside Mark's slick back passage. Steve attempted to fit all of Mark inside his mouth, drawing up and down his entire length. Beside him, Jack nibbled Mark's neck and ear, whispering, "Come, you gorgeous angel. Come."

Instantly lit up, Mark tensed his legs and back, reaching out his arms for something to hold while he spun. Jack grabbed his hand and held tight.

Mark let go a loud, whimpering moan of euphoria as his lover sucked him down to the root.

The blast to his loins astonished him. It was so intense he felt his eyes fluttering under his eyelids. "Ah! Ah, oh, sweet Mother of God."

As he gasped, Mark managed to open his eyes. Three men were smiling adoringly at him. "Oh, God." A wave of emotion washed through him. When he started sobbing, he was covered in male bodies.

"What is it, Mark?" Jack asked in anxiety.

"I'm so happy." Mark dabbed at his eyes. "You're all so wonderful to me."

"Sweetie," Steve crooned, kissing his chin, "you're the amazing one."

"Thank you." Mark blubbered like a baby. "Adam...thank

you."

"My pleasure. I never thought I'd do this, but it was awesome."

"Stevie..."

"Yes, my love."

"You're the best boyfriend a man could ever have."

"I know what makes you happy." Steve squeezed him tight.

"You okay, Jackie?"

"More than okay, Mark."

"Adam?"

"Doing fine."

"Good. I like to keep all my men happy." Mark smiled.

Chapter Sixteen

It was the morning after and Mark was in Adam's guest bedroom. He yawned and stretched lazily. Steve's warm body was beside him, so Mark snuggled against him, reminiscing about their fantastic night together. It had been perfect. He and Jack finally connected, Adam wasn't upset or jealous, and Steve's generosity as a lover overwhelmed him.

Like a cat, Mark purred in contentment, snaking his arms and legs around Steve and nestling against his neck. Steve stirred at the touch.

When he opened his bright blue eyes, Mark shivered, madly in love. "Hey, handsome."

"Morning." Steve stretched his back, yawning.

"Some night, huh?" Mark writhed on him.

A soft smile played across Steve's lips. "Amazing."

"Want to play so we can shower and see what our men are up to?"

Steve wrapped Mark up in his arms and squeezed him tight. "Oh, yes…"

Mark reached between Steve's legs and drew his cock through his fingers. "Morning blowjob?"

"I have a better idea. Let's do it in the shower."

"Perfect." Mark threw the sheet off and scampered to the

bathroom with Steve in hot pursuit.

"Code three!" Steve laughed, grabbing at Mark playfully.

"Lights and sirens!" Mark broke up with hilarity.

Steve cuddled his arms around him and picked him up off the floor. "Roger. Ten-Four."

In his white slacks, shirtless and barefoot, holding Steve's hand, Mark descended the stairs to find Jack and Adam in the kitchen. "Good morning," Mark greeted them cheerfully.

"Coffee," Steve moaned, finding a mug and pouring both him and Mark a cup. "Bagels?"

"Yup." Adam sliced a few in half, setting them on a plate. "Help yourself."

"How are you both? Any morning-after regrets?" Mark asked, walking behind Adam and pulling his hair into a ponytail as Adam set out smoked salmon and cream cheese.

Adam peeked over his shoulder at Mark. "Do you?"

"No." Mark combed his fingers through Adam's locks. "Steve? Will you grow your hair for me?"

"No." Steve laughed, sitting down at the counter.

"Bullocks." Mark stuck his tongue out at him.

"Have a seat, Mark. Jack, Steve, dig in."

They each took a stool at the large marble-topped island and began making sandwiches.

"Jack?"

"Yes, Steve?" Jack spread cream cheese on his poppy-seed bagel.

"Do you have that book of male nudes Mark was in? I ordered it, but I haven't gotten my copy yet."

"I do." Jack's light eyes gleamed.

"Uh, can I see it?" Steve chuckled at Jack's demonic expression.

"I haven't even seen it," Adam added, chewing his food.

"Are you hiding it, Jackie?" Mark licked cream cheese off his finger.

"No. No one's ever expressed an interest in it. I'll get it after breakfast."

"Cool." Steve grinned slyly at Mark.

Once they had cleared up the dishes, Jack disappeared from the room. When he returned, he held a large, hardbound book aloft.

"Yes!" Steve rushed to meet him.

"Have a seat in the living room." Jack gestured to the sofa.

Mark meandered in, still sipping a cup of coffee as Jack and Steve sat down together on the couch.

"Did he find it?" Adam asked, standing behind Mark.

"Yes."

"Oh. Cool." Adam brushed passed him and dropped down alongside Steve, who held the book on his lap.

"Where is he?" Steve leafed through the pages.

"Uh…" Jack flipped a few pages. "Here's one."

The three men inspected the book. Steve was the first to look up. "Oh, Mark."

"Good?" Mark moved closer, gazing down at it. It was the one where he was in a bed, the sheet at his pubic hair.

"Next." Steve waited as Jack continued to search.

This time Adam peeked up at Mark. "Christ, Richfield."

"Insta-wood." Steve shifted on the couch.

"Look at that fantastic stallion." Jack pointed.

"Is that the one with Dedra Dunn?" Mark peeked down at it.

"I wasn't talking about the horse," Jack quipped.

Steve and Adam chuckled, exchanging glances.

"There's one of just his torso." Jack flipped pages. "That one."

Steve and Adam moaned in harmony. Mark leaned over to have a look.

"Nice ass, Richfield," Adam said. "Holy crap."

"Oh, to be twenty-one again." Mark sighed.

"Shut the fuck up." Steve narrowed his eyes at his lover. "You look the same."

"Don't I wish." Mark set his mug on the coffee table.

"Last one." Jack shuffled pages.

"You know them all by heart?" Steve asked in amusement.

"Of course." Jack pointed.

A collective groan was his reply.

"Is that the one in the shower, Jackie?" Mark tried to see it upside down.

"Yes."

"They're beautiful photos, Mark." Adam gazed up at him. "It's nice having a memento of your youthful beauty."

Mark's mood darkened, knowing it would fade, was fading.

"I can't wait to get my copy." Steve smoothed his hand over the photo greedily.

"Did you get that other photo copied yet, Mark?" Jack asked. "Mark?"

Mark turned away, moving through the kitchen to the sliding doors and the ocean. Once he stepped out to the breeze and heard the cresting waves, tears stung his eyes.

He was soon joined by three worried men.

"What's wrong, baby?" Steve touched his cheek.

What would he have to offer them once his looks faded? Mark shuddered to think of that day.

"Mark?" Jack reached for his hand.

"Nothing. I'm fine." Mark put on a brave smile.

Adam gripped Mark's arms to meet his eyes. "There's more to you than your looks."

"Stop being perceptive, Adam. You shouldn't know me that well already."

"I've been telling him that for years." Steve sighed.

"So have I. Two fucking decades." Jack shook his head.

With both his arms, Adam wrapped Mark in an embrace, rocking him. "You're being silly. You know how much those two guys love you? They don't give a shit about anything but you."

"Now," Mark whimpered sadly.

"Maaark!" Steve groaned.

"Never mind." Mark perked up, parting from Adam's hug. "So, what do we do today, gentlemen?"

"Come back inside." Adam slid the door open.

Several hands guided Mark into the kitchen. Steve stood behind him, holding his shoulders and resting his chin on him. "You're too hung up on your looks."

"No. Quite the contrary. Everyone else is." Mark knew he was bringing them down and felt terrible. "I just want to always be fuckable."

Adam stifled a laugh. "You always will be."

"Promise?"

"Promise." Adam touched his cheek.

Steve jammed his hips into Mark's behind. "As long as he keeps getting it up the ass he'll be happy."

Jack shook his head, smiling. "Believe me, Mark, you will get it in the end. All the way to the bitter end."

"Good. Make it a vow." Mark held up his hand.

They acknowledged it, holding up their hands.

"I…" Mark began. "Say your names."

They did, trying not to laugh at him.

"Will always want to make love to Mark Antonious Richfield." Mark waited as they repeated it. "Even when he is ninety." All three men repeated it, obviously holding back their roars of hilarity. "Good. I shall hold you to it."

Steve grabbed him roughly in a headlock from behind, wrestling with him playfully. "You're a nut!"

"A fantastic nut," Adam said.

"I knew that back in ninety-three." Jack returned to the living room.

"He did." Mark nodded emphatically. "He knows I've a screw loose."

"And he still loves you. Imagine that," Steve said.

Mark met Jack and Adam in the living room. "What now?"

"Another day in the continuing saga of Mark Richfield." Adam sat on the couch, crossing his legs.

"The never-ending story." Jack joined Adam, leaning against him.

"Never a dull moment." Steve hugged Mark from behind.

"No. No one could say I've had a dull life." Mark held Steve's arms tight. "And at least I'm loved."

"You are." Steve kissed his hair.

"That's all that counts." Mark smiled adoringly at his fan club. "That's all that counts."

"As long as you get it in the end, eh, hot stuff?"

"Come here, copper." Mark reached out for him.

Steve cuddled him in his embrace. "I love you."

"I love you, too." Mark stared into Steve's blue eyes. "Forever."

"Forever," Steve echoed, kissing him.

Getting It In The End

The End

About the Author

Award-winning author G. A. Hauser was born in Fair Lawn, New Jersey, USA, and attended university in New York City. She moved to Seattle, Washington where she worked as a patrol officer with the Seattle Polic Department. In early 2000 G.A. moved to Hertfordshire, England, where she began her writing in earnest and published her first book, *In the Shadow of Alexander*. Now a full-time writer in Ohio, G.A. has written dozens of novels, including several bestsellers of gay fiction. For more information on other books by G.A., visit the author at her official website at: www.authorgahauser.com.

G.A. has won awards from All Romance eBooks for Best Novel 2007, *Secrets and Misdemeanors*, Best Author 2007. Best Novel 2008, *Mile High*, and Best Author 2008.

The G.A. Hauser Collection

Available Now
Single Titles

Unnecessary Roughness

Got Men?

Heart of Steele

All Man

Julian

Black Leather Phoenix

In the Dark and What Should Never Be, Erotic Short Stories

Mark and Sharon (formerly titled A Question of Sex)

A Man's Best Friend

It Takes a Man

The Physician and the Actor

For Love and Money

The Kiss

Naked Dragon

Secrets and Misdemeanors

Capital Games

Giving Up the Ghost

To Have and To Hostage

Love you, Loveday

The Boy Next Door

When Adam Met Jack

Exposure
The Vampire and the Man-eater
Murphy's Hero
Mark Antonious deMontford
Prince of Servitude
Calling Dr. Love
The Rape of St. Peter
The Wedding Planner
Going Deep
Double Trouble
Pirates
Miller's Tale
Vampire Nights
Teacher's Pet
In the Shadow of Alexander
The Rise and Fall of the Sacred Band of Thebes

The Action Series
Acting Naughty
Playing Dirty
Getting it in the End
Behaving Badly
Dripping Hot
Packing Heat

Men in Motion Series
Mile High
Cruising
Driving Hard
Leather Boys

G.A. Hauser
Writing as Amanda Winters

9 781449 592974